Laurence E Dahners

ISBN: 978-1477629635
ASIN: B005ORQO7W

Quicker

An Ell Donsaii story #1

Laurence E Dahners

Author's Note

This book is the first of the series, the "Ell Donsaii stories."

Other Books and Series by Laurence E Dahners

Series

The Hyllis Family series
The Vaz series
The Bonesetter series
The Blindspot series
The Proton Field series

Single books (not in series)

The Transmuter's Daughter
Six Bits
Shy Kids Can Make Friends Too

For the most up to date information go to

Laury.Dahners.com/stories.html

Table of Contents

Author's Note 4
Preprologue 7
Prologue 9
Chapter One 20
Chapter Two 49
Chapter Three 85
Chapter Four 109
Chapter Five 125
Chapter Six 149
Chapter Seven 167
Chapter Eight 215
Epilogue 238
Author's Afterword 241
Acknowledgements 243

Preprologue

Ell's father, Allan Donsaii, was an unusually gifted quarterback. Startlingly strong, and a phenomenally accurate passer, during his college career he finished two full seasons without any interceptions and two games with 100 percent completions. Unfortunately, he wasn't big enough to be drafted by the pros.

Extraordinarily quick, Ell's mother, Kristen Taylor captained her college soccer team and rarely played a game without a steal.

Allan and Kristen dated

more and more seriously through college, marrying at the end of their senior year. Their friends teased them that they'd only married in order to start their own sports dynasty.

Their daughter Ell got Kristen's quickness, magnified by Allan's surprising strength and highly accurate coordination.

She also has a new mutation that affects the myelin sheaths of her nerves. This mutation produces nerve transmission speeds nearly double those of normal neurons. With faster nerve impulse transmission, she has far quicker reflexes. Yet her new type of myelin sheath is also thinner, allowing more axons, and therefore more neurons, to be packed into the same sized skull. These two factors result in a brain with more neurons, though it isn't larger, and a faster processing speed, akin to a computer with a smaller, faster CPU architecture.

Most importantly, under the influence of adrenalin in a fight or flight situation, her nerves transmit even more rapidly than their normally remarkable speed.

Much more rapidly…

Prologue

Thinking, *I'd like some of that,* Joe watched the pretty waitress walk toward him.

Just my type, he mused, reddish hair, slender, nice legs.

She'd said something, he realized.

"Would you like a refill on your drink?" she asked again.

Joe let his eyes slowly pass down her body then back up. He lifted an eyebrow and gave her his "sexy" smile. "I'd like a long drink of you." Her pale green eyes frosted over at the comment. He shrugged, "But I'd settle for some Coke."

"Coming right up." She said in a strained tone. It sounded like she'd tried—though failed—to sound bright and cheerful.

Bitch, he thought to himself as she turned and strode off to the battered counter of the little cafe. *Thinks she's too good for me.* Her long graceful stride kept his eye though. She didn't wiggle when she walked, nonetheless, her tight little butt looked great in the pleated mini skirt.

Joe seethed inside. Nonetheless, when she returned, he smiled and tried again. "Hey, thanks for the drink honey. What time do you get off work?"

Her eyes, cool before this sortie, went cold. "Sorry, married and have a kid." There was a long pause. Then with a taut smile, "But it's nice that you're interested."

Yeah, right, he thought, *"nice that I'm interested." Bitch just wants a tip... I'll give her a tip all right.* Fuming inside, he had his AI pay his check without a tip, left a single penny on the table, picked up his shades and headed out to his car. It was as he was about to get in that he saw the sign in the window of the small seaside joint. "Open 11AM to 9PM." *Damn*, he thought, *it's already 8:45*.

I'm gonna have some fun, he decided. He walked to the front of the car and opened the frunk. Heat from the long summer day billowed out at him. He rummaged through his duffle, pushing aside a bundle of $100s to find his black Levis, a black long sleeved shirt and black sneakers. He went back into the little restaurant's bathroom, changed, and then strode back out to sit in his car and wait for the woman to leave.

~~~

He nearly missed her. She went out the back door of the restaurant, beyond his line of sight. But then he recognized her getting into the old clunker two cars down from his own. To his surprise he heard an old gas engine crank. Her little blue Toyota backed out of its space and turned out of the gravel lot, trailing a small cloud of dust. His black Ford, already turned on for the AC, whirred out of its space and turned to follow her. In a few minutes the two cars were rolling over the bridge from Emerald Isle to Morehead City.

She turned into one of the shabby, older residential areas of the town. Joe lagged farther back, but still saw which driveway she pulled into. He drove past, picking the number off the mailbox and parked just around the corner. "Sammy?" he said to his AI (Artificial Intelligence).

"Yes?" her contralto responded in his ear.

"Who lives at 319 West Garson Street, Morehead
~~~

City, North Carolina?"

There was a momentary pause while the AI searched the net. "Kristen Donsaii, age 33 and her daughter Ell, age 11."

"What about a husband?"

Another pause. "Allan Donsaii, died six years ago in a boating accident."

Yeah right. Sure you're married bitch! Joe snarled to himself. He put on his black gloves, picked up his cap, and got out of his Ford, starting toward the woman's house. To his surprise, just as he got to the beginning of the faded picket fence in front of her little clapboard house, she stepped out the door in jogging shorts. She headed down the walk without recognizing him, opening her gate right after he walked past it, then turned and jogged off down the street the opposite direction. Joe turned around to admire her slender, muscular legs as they flashed off in the fading sunlight. Her bouncing ponytail caught his attention for a moment. *Dumb as a post,* he thought to himself, *running at twilight*. He walked around the block as the light faded further. When he came back past her place, he hopped over the little fence, strode up to the porch and stepped into the shadows of the vine covered trellis beside the door. He put on the black stocking hat and pulled it down over his face. After a moment he thought, *Damn, it's too hot for this!* But, immobile and covered in black, he knew he'd be hard to see in the dim light.

Joe stood quietly sweating, listening for the sound of a TV, but hearing nothing. *Kid must be out,* he thought to himself. *Or maybe just on her AI.* He shrugged, *Doesn't really matter.*

It seemed like forever before he heard the tapping

sound of the woman's feet coming back down the sidewalk. Joe stilled himself as she came around the corner, stepped through her gate and trudged up the walk. He waited until she'd turned the key in her lock, surprised to realize she was so poor she didn't even have a door AI.

As the door swung open Joe stepped in behind her, grabbed her by the ponytail, ripped her AI off her head hard enough to unjack it, and forced her through the opening. She stumbled and fell forward. Joe crashed down on top, driving the breath out of her.

With a thrill he noticed how her body felt nice and firm.

There was a little shriek from across the room. Hauling back on the bitch's ponytail with his right hand, Joe straightened his mask with the left and looked over to see a kid sitting on a worn couch, her head tipped back to gape at him from under her AI's HUD (Heads Up Display). "You'll keep quiet if you want your Mommy to stay alive," Joe snarled. The kid stared at him with wide eyes.

The bitch under Joe gasped a breath and wheezed, "Run Ell! Run!"

Joe hauled back on the ponytail, "Run, and I'll break your mommy's scrawny neck! Pull off that AI!" The little girl slowly pulled off her AI's headband, disconnected the jack from its beltpack and set it aside.

Joe rose to one knee, forcing it into the bitch's back. He dug in his satchel for his duct tape. "Put your left hand back here." The woman started to struggle and he clapped her hard on the side of the head. He leaned down to whisper in her ear, "I'm gonna do *you* in any case. But if you make it hard for me—I'll do your *daughter* as a bonus." She slumped, putting her arm back. He wound the wrist with duct tape. "Now the right one." Shaking in reaction she put her right arm back by her left and he bound her wrists together.

Joe looked up. To his surprise the skinny reddish-blond kid was right in front of him, trembling like a leaf. He'd expected to see her cowering on the couch. *Well, this certainly simplifies things.* Sitting up on her mother's back he said, "Gimme your left hand kid."

It wasn't her left hand that moved, but rather her right.

Impossibly fast, that hand, like a striking snake.

Two fingers spread out to go on each side of his nose.

They plunged into his eyeballs, her sharp little nails puncturing the sclera and bursting the globes like grapes struck by arrows.

Joe reared back, clapping his hand over his ruined eyes and scrabbling backwards out the door by feel alone.

~~~

When the policemen came, he was still staggering through the unending dark, searching for his car.

***

Jamal turned to Aki and said, "I think we're too close. That gun sounds like it's just over the rocks."

Aki stood on his tiptoes. Thirteen, he'd just hit his growth spurt. He'd always wanted be first on the scene so he could see more of every exciting thing that happened in their war torn little world. "Help me up," he said," give me a foot. I want to know what those
~~~

American devils are doing over there."

Reluctantly, Jamal bent, clasped his hands and gave Aki a boost. Aki skinned up the rock and raised his head over the edge, looking around in delight. Jamal heard a knocking sound. His temper flared as he felt Aki spit on the back of his down turned neck. He released Aki's foot and stood up shouting in anger, then bemusement as Aki dropped, not just to his feet to bounce around boasting of his exploits, but all the way to the ground.

Aki lay rigidly twitching, his hands twisted into backward fists. Jamal dreamily noted that Aki's head was misshapen.

Jamal wiped the back of his own neck and came away with blood. Absently he noticed splatters of blood *everywhere* around them. He bent over Aki's quivering form and saw a splatter of blood on his forehead.

No, it was a *hole*. Jamal reached toward the hole.

Suddenly he noticed Aki's bulging, lifeless eyes.

~~~

Jamal was running, running, running.

~~~

It seemed as if Jamal'd been running forever, but it was actually only a few hundred meters to his house. He stepped into the small mud brick shack he'd shared with his mother and Grandfather since his father'd been killed in the fighting. The adults were both at work. Even during a war you had to eat, and this war, though fluctuating in intensity, had been a constant in the family's life since long before the Americans had arrived to take up one side of the conflict. Jamal went to his hiding place, an old wooden crate in the corner that served them as a table. He turned it away from the wall and, folding himself up, sat down and pulled it back over him. Not having hidden in it for quite some time, he found it'd gotten much tighter than it used to be.

Jamal sat while his breathing slowed and the racing in his mind calmed. After a bit he had settled and began to think about getting out of the box and going for help. Someone should tell Aki's mother. But then Jamal heard more firing. It sounded like it was on the street outside! Jamal huddled back down, squinting out through cracks in the box. He could only see the narrow confines of the room. Despite the heat he shivered, queasy waves rolling over him as he thought back on his friend. His mind's eye brought up Aki's smiling, grinning face, always full of devilment, now the lifeless husk he'd last seen lying in the blood splattered dirt. Though, as a man, he knew he shouldn't show fear, he quietly sobbed in terror.

Someone ran into the room! In mid sob Jamal closed his throat and made no further sound. He peered though the cracks. *Mother*! Jamal weakly reached to move the crate he hid beneath. But then another shadow entered the room. *A soldier!* Jamal shrank back in terror at the beetle-helmeted horror that'd entered their small dwelling. Jamal's mind gibbered as the soldier grasped his mother by the shoulder and spun her about, ripping her clothing. She fell to the floor and the soldier fell on top of her, forcing his way between her kicking legs. Jamal felt warm urine pouring into his own crotch as he reached out to push away the crate with watery arms.

Then he saw his Grandfather step into the room with one of their kitchen knives. To Jamal's great admiration, the frail old man advanced with sudden vitality toward the struggling couple on the floor and quickly dropped, plunging the knife into the soldier's back.

But it didn't plunge! It stopped, point barely penetrating the soldier's armored backplate. Propelled by all the force he could muster, the old man's hand slid off the handle and down over the blade, lacerating his fingers as it slid. With a shout that must have been a curse, the soldier rolled off Jamal's mother and away from his grandfather. A pistol appeared in the soldier's hand and barked twice at Grandfather, then swung to Jamal's mother where it barked once.

The soldier stuffed his obscenely swollen organ back in his pants and was struggling to his feet when another beetle helmeted soldier burst in through the doorway. "What happened?"

"Tryin' to question these frags when they attacked me! Sunsabitches!"

The second soldier looked for a moment at Mother's bare legs. Briefly Jamal thought he'd question the story he'd been told. But then the soldier simply shrugged, looked back over his shoulder and said, "Let's get outta here."

The two soldiers hustled out of the door, leaving Jamal desolate and alone.

No family.

No friends.

No life.

Just an upwelling bleak hatred.

***

Jamal stood staring at distant heat mirages through the chain link fence around the refugee compound. A small voice came from behind him. "Jamal, there's a man wants to talk to you."

He turned and saw Aki's sister. For a moment he saw his friend's smiling likeness in her face, but her face sagged with no hint of Aki's sparkle. He thought back, trying to remember if she'd always been this way? Or just since Aki and her father had died? She started to turn away and Jamal realized he should answer her. "What's he want?"

"He's talking to boys who don't have families."

Jamal wandered to the little table where the man sat near the entrance to the compound. The man, obscenely fat, sweated profusely and wiped at his head with a cloth that had probably once been white. Jamal instinctively disliked him. "What do you want?"

"You've lost all of your family?"

"Yes."

"And you hate the Americans for their part in your tragedy?"

"Yes."

"Do you want revenge?"

Jamal stared. *Revenge? Of course, but how?* Nonetheless, "Yes."

The man stared into Jamal's eyes. "You might be killed… or called upon to die."

"I don't care." Jamal spit into the dust. *What do I have to live for?*

The fat man stared into Jamal's eyes a few moments longer, then shook his head as if frightened by what he saw. He wiped his head again then stood. "Come."

***

"I, will, not, study, that, accursed, language!" Jamal's eyes were slits and he could barely control his trembling fury. "All these things you want to teach me are worthless. They won't help me kill Americans! Just give me a gun and send me into a city! Or give me a bomb and I..."

The blow cut him off in mid sentence. Jamal flew from the stool he'd been sitting on and crashed against the dusty mud-brick wall. Head ringing, Jamal looked up into a face somehow all the more fearsome for not appearing angry. "Little one," the man who'd struck Jamal shook his head. "Our plan is not to *waste* you, just to kill one, or two, or even fifty Americans. Oh no, you will be *much* more deadly than that. A *great* warrior does not kill a few of the enemy through brute strength, he kills *thousands* through cunning. At the moment you have *no* cunning. We'll teach you canniness, and deceit, and strategy. We'll fashion you into a weapon much more dangerous than the Americans' vaunted smart weapons. For now though, you are a 'dumb weapon,' one who's too stupid to even know how little it comprehends." The man squatted down, bringing his face within a few inches of Jamal's. Jamal shrank away from his garlicky breath and coarsely pitted skin. "You will learn what we *tell* you to learn, *when* we tell you to learn it, and you'll *stop* your whining!"

~~~

Thus, Jamal set about learning English, and eventually many other things he thought unimportant. But he never again complained. Not even when he found, years later and to his great amazement, that he was being sent to the accursed America to study at a
~~~

university there.

Chapter One

Ell's AI chimed in her ear, "You have a call from Mr. Mandal."

Mandal was her school counselor. Ell said, "I'll take it... Yes Mr. Mandal?"

Mandal's voice came on, "Ell, your SAT scores have come in, I assume you've seen them?"

"Yeah, my writing score sucked."

Mandal chuckled, "Ell, you maxed out the math section! I wasn't even aware that they gave 100th percentile scores until *you* got one! I checked with the testing people and it means you got the highest score in the country. In other words, that it was better than 100 percent, or *all*, of the other test takers. I'm certain this is the first time anyone in our school district got the high score in the country. And as a sophomore you can take the SAT again next year and focus on getting a better score on the writing section."

"But I want to go for early admission."

There was a pause. "Can you come in and talk about it? I'll look into what your options might be."

"Come in?" Ell couldn't imagine what they couldn't handle over a link.

"Yeah, we should talk, 'off the record.'"

~~~

The next morning Ell was in Mandal's office and they
~~~

both unjacked their AIs. "So, what's the rush to get off to college?"

She shrugged, "I just want to get out of *here*."

Mandal scratched his chin. He knew that Ell's mother had remarried a couple of years ago. "Trouble at home?"

Ell shrugged dismissively. "No."

"Your step dad, what's his name again?"

She grimaced, "Jake Radford."

"Mr. Radford causing you any trouble?"

"He's a jerk. But it isn't anything I can't handle."

Mandal looked at her hard. "Is he doing anything to you?"

"No! I don't like the way he looks at me. But he's harmless. I just can't believe my mother married him is all."

"You're sure?"

"Yes! Talk to me about colleges."

Mandal looked at her pensively for a few more moments. The girl had brilliant green eyes, short, silky, strawberry blond hair and a smooth unblemished complexion with a light sprinkling of freckles on an evenly proportioned, "pixie like" face. Slender, brilliant and an athletic phenom, she could easily get a softball or volleyball scholarship. However, she'd already told him that she wanted to focus on academics in college. "Do you have money for private or out of state schools?" Mandal knew her mom was a schoolteacher and doubted they had a lot of savings, but maybe there was insurance money from her father's death. Or possibly the step-dad had money?

"No. In-state'll be hard enough. You don't think I could get a scholarship?

"Athletic?"

"No."

"Well your scores would get you *some* kind of scholarship. To be honest you probably could get a great scholarship if you'd get involved in some leadership activities and pull up that writing score on the SAT."

"No! I want out of here by the end of next year and I *don't* want to run for office. It's hard enough being two years younger than my classmates without making a target out of myself by running against Mindy Martin."

Mandal sat back, feeling uncertain. Ell's apparent shyness and feelings of social inadequacy always surprised him. Whenever he met with her, she acted as if no one liked her. His personal take on the school's social dynamics placed her among the most popular kids in the school.

She might be chronologically younger than her classmates but she acted more mature than most of them. She didn't seem to belong to any cliques, but *he* thought she was liked by kids from all strata. He was sure her stunning looks contributed to her popularity—except perhaps with the country club clique of fashionable girls who might be jealous. Anyway, Mandal didn't *think* she acted "better than thou" like a lot of the other pretty girls did.

He wasn't even sure she *understood* how beautiful she was. In any case, her humility regarding her sports accomplishments and her willingness to help *anyone* with *any* problem had to be a huge part of it too. Besides, just her athleticism guaranteed that she'd be admired, especially since she wasn't a glory hound. He wondered if she thought she wasn't popular *because* she didn't belong to any of the cliques.

He decided to try once more, "I'm pretty sure you'd

have a good chance at being elected to office—"

"Hah!" She interrupted, "Not a chance. You really have *no* idea what it's like."

Well, he admitted to himself, *that's true; I really* don't *know what goes on inside the kids' social structure.* Kids loved by teachers were sometimes despised by their peers without the teachers knowing it.

"Okay then. Carolina? I'm almost certain you could get in. I doubt you'd get a full ride scholarship like the Morehead without doing some of the things I've mentioned though."

"No, State. I want to study engineering. Well, maybe physics."

"It's a good school. You could apply for the Park scholarship, but I really don't think you'd get it based on your grades and a record setting math score alone."

"I can *apply* to both schools *and* for both scholarships though right?"

"Sure."

"Do any private or out of state schools have full ride scholarships?"

"I'll look into it for you. Would you consider a military academy?"

A wrinkle formed between Ell's eyebrows. "Military?"

"West Point, Navy, Air Force Academy. They provide full rides to *all* their students, but you'd owe them some time on active duty afterward. Great educations though, and they're all big on engineering."

"Huh," she said thoughtfully, "I'll look them up on the net."

~~~
~~~

Kristen heard Ell come in the front door. "Ell? Did you get your SAT results today?"

"Yes, Mom."

"Well?" Kristen said with the patiently exasperated tone of a parent having to drag conversation out of her teenager.

"I got 94th percentile on reading but only 78th on writing."

"Ell, those aren't bad! Especially for a sophomore... Wait, how'd you do on math?"

"I got 100th percentile on math."

"Hundredth?! What's that mean? I don't know the scoring system, but how can anyone get the *hundredth* percentile?"

"Um, it's the max score. It means that I had the highest score of all test takers this year."

"Really?! The max score for all sophomores?"

"No... all takers."

"My God, Ell! That's wonderful! I knew you were good at math but... holy crap!" She paused and frowned, "How are you *that* good at math when the Carteret schools don't even have any AP classes for you to take?"

"You can take AP classes online. They're expensive if you take them for credit but you can audit almost any of them for free." She shrugged, "I *really* like math. After I got interested in it I audited the online AP courses and then some free online college courses. The courses had a lot of recommended reading and most of that was pretty cool too."

Kristen stared, "How did you have time to do that between your sports and school stuff?"

"Just here and there, it doesn't take all that long to get through a course." *Especially when you can't sleep at night and really like a subject,* Ell thought.

Kristen stood stunned for a moment, wondering how her daughter could just breeze through advanced math courses without any help and tell her, *"they don't take long."* She shook her head to cast off the uncertainty, then threw her arms around her daughter, "Oh, Ell! You make me so proud! We've got to go out and celebrate!" That got Ell into her mother's excitement and the two grinned at one another for a moment. "Just wait till Jake gets home."

Ell's frame of mind slumped. She'd been excited to go out and celebrate with her mom. *Not* with Jake. She had a feeling he'd ruin her good mood somehow. Ell heard the back door creak open. "I'm home." Jake called out. He stepped into the room and frowned, "What are you guys all excited about?"

Kristen beamed, "Ell got a hundredth percentile on the math section of the SAT?"

Jake's brow drew down further, "*That's* not possible."

Ell wondered whether he meant there was no such score or that it couldn't be possible his stepdaughter got such a good score. Kristen grinned though and said, "I'd never heard of a 'hundredth-percentile' score either, but Ell says it's the highest score of all takers this year, meaning that she did better than 100% of the other people who took the SAT!"

Jake shook his head and said, "That can't be right. Forward your result to my AI." His tone was suspicious and peremptory.

Ell stared at him for a moment as ice ran down her spine and she felt her right eyelid twitch involuntarily a few times. Then she said, "No." Her resentment over a hundred little put downs from Jake over the past two years had just boiled over.

"What?!"

"I said no. You can trust me or not, but they're *my* results and I'm *not* forwarding them to *you*." Ell heart throbbed and she worried that she might get too wound up. Some bad things could happen when she got overexcited. She still had nightmares about blinding the man who'd attacked her mother three years ago. She looked down at the floor and took a couple of deep, calming breaths.

Kristen looked at her in shock. "Ell!" She'd often been uneasy about the rude way Jake talked to her daughter, but Ell had always let it roll off her in the past. Kristen had wondered if her uneasiness about his condescension was just an overreaction. After all, mothers are often overprotective of their children.

Ell felt calmer. She looked her mother in the eye. "Sorry Mom. You love him, but I don't and I'm sick of his attitude toward me."

Jake had turned bright red with fury. "Look young lady. I don't give a crap how you feel about my attitude. But if you want to go to college, you're going to have to do things *my* way. Send. Me. Those. Scores!"

Ell's pulse throbbed harder. She took another deep calming breath. "No." She felt her lip involuntarily curl, "*You* can't keep me from going to college."

Jake strode across the room to tower over Ell, "Who do *you* think's going to pay for you to go to college? Your mom? *She* doesn't have the money!"

Ell felt herself going over the edge into the bad place rage could take her. She took another deep breath to try to calm herself but this one didn't seem to help much. "I don't *want* your money, *asshole*!" Her own mind gibbered at her. She *never* spoke this way to adults. *Get control of yourself!* she thought.

The world had slowed down and everything had started moving in a dreamlike fashion, the way it had when the man attacked her mom. She had queasy flashbacks to the feeling of her fingers bursting into the guy's eyeballs. She'd only meant to poke his eyes to distract him.

Ell noticed with dismay that her mother looked mortified. Kristen had started crying. Then Ell saw Jake's shoulder tense. His arm swung back, and then forward, hand open. With everything moving in slow motion Ell, understood he was going to slap her.

Her mind projected his hand's intended trajectory, and—because the world seemed like it was moving in a slow, molasses-like fashion—that made it easy to duck down out of the path his hand was taking toward her head. As it missed her, she realized that the powerful, un-deflected slap was going to go on to hit her mother instead!

Ell punched up into the underside of his forearm with her right first, striking just above the wrist. She was trying to deflect his hand up over her mother's head as well. *Oh no!* she thought to herself as agony washed up her arm from her hand. Moving so quickly, she'd hit his wrist *far* too hard! Every time she had a fight or flight reaction like she was currently experiencing, the world seemed to move so slowly—and Ell moved *so* quickly—that she overdid things.

She saw a visible dent appear in the flesh just proximal to Jake's wrist. Shock waves spread from and bounced back across the site where Ell's hand had struck. Though it'd seemed like a slow bump to Ell when she did it, she could tell now that it had been a really hard strike. She saw the effect of the blow on Jake, as he spun clumsily from the momentum of his unexpectedly missed slap.

His eyebrows initially rose in surprise when he failed to make contact, then twitched together in concern. A moment later they rose again as pain messages from his wrist flooded into his brain.

Jake and Ell both grasped their injured appendages and bent over with the pain, glaring at each other.

~~~

Ell lay on her bed staring up into her HUD. Jake hadn't been able to use his hand after their little incident so Kristen had taken him to the ER. Since they'd left, Ell's mind had wandered over, around and through the disaster that'd just befallen her little family. She'd distracted herself by vigorously researching scholarship and military academy options. She swore she' to herself that d pay her own way through college even if she had to work a few years before she attended and live like a pauper while she was there. The door creaked open downstairs as her mother and Jake come in. Ell got out of bed and went to the top of the stairs where she stood uncomfortably, waiting with her arms crossed and her painful right hand squeezed in her armpit. The bases of her fingers had turned black and blue. She wondered if she might have done her hand serious damage, but, despite the pain, it seemed to work okay. When Kristen and Jake came out from the kitchen Ell said, "I'm sorry."

They looked up at her. Ell's mother looked concerned. Jake, wearing a cast, still looked pissed. "You *broke* my ulna!" He said in a tone carrying a mixture of anger and astonishment.

"You... you tried to slap me!" Ell's tone was low,
~~~

words uttered through gritted teeth, but there could be no mistaking the rage in her voice. She had thought that *surely* he would apologize to her as well, especially if she went first. Even though he never apologized for anything, surely he would apologize for trying to *hit* her?

"Hey! Hey..." Kristen made little downward pushing motions with her hands, trying to calm them both.

Ell's vision blurred with tears. A sense of abandonment swept over her as she realized her mother wasn't taking her side. She turned and strode back to her room, picking up the suitcase that she'd already packed. When she reached the top of the stairs she saw Jake and her mother having a quiet but heated argument. They looked up at her standing calmly with her suitcase. "Good!" Jake said beneath lowered brows.

"What? Where are you going?" Kristen asked, wide-eyed.

"Gram's. I *can't* stay here." Ell started down the stairs.

Tears streamed down Kristen's face, but with resignation she quietly said, "Okay, I'll take you," and picked up her purse.

~~~

After she pulled out of the driveway, Kristen said, "Ell?" When there was no response she said, "Ell, I'm sure you feel I've let you down. I feel the same way. But I really have no idea *what* to do when the two people I love hate each other like you and Jake seem to." She paused, hoping Ell might comment, but the girl sat, arms crossed, staring stonily ahead. "Ell, if you and Jake can't live together... If you can't live together, I think having you at Gram's is the best way to keep our family
~~~

from coming apart. I know he acts like a jerk sometimes and I'm going to talk to him about it. But you were pretty rude to him too."

"Only after he'd been rude to me for the *thousandth* time."

"Well I do appreciate your apologizing to him. I'll talk to him about apologizing to you and maybe you can move back home in a couple of days?"

"*He*... he will *never* apologize. I, therefore, will never live in that house again."

Silence reigned the rest of the way to Gram Taylor's house. When Gram saw Ell with a suitcase she clapped her hands to her face, eyes darting back and forth from Kristen to Ell, as she took in their grim looks, "Oh! I was afraid this would happen one day." She looked at Ell, "You and Jake get in a fight?"

"Yes Gram. I'm sorry, but I'm hoping you'll let me live with you for a while?"

"Of course, of course." Ell's grandmother shepherded Ell into the house and began bustling around, clearing drawers in the spare room and throwing their contents on the bed, "I'm sure you guys will work it out after a bit."

"Not gonna happen Gram," Ell said stiffly. "If I can't stay with you till I go away to school next fall, I'll need to look into other arrangements."

"Sure, sure. Stay as long as you like. Keep me from being lonely! Next fall? You're just a rising Junior. You mean the fall after the coming one?"

"No Gram, I'm going to apply for early admission and go after my Junior year."

Gram's eyes went back and forth from Ell to Kristen and back again, "Really? Will you be able to get in?"

Kristen said quietly, "Mom, she got the highest score

in the *country* on her math SAT."

Gram clapped her hands together in delight. "Oh! That's great! Let's celebrate with ice cream!"

They all worked to bag the erstwhile contents of the drawers for placement in Gram's storage closet and then spent a few moments unpacking the meager contents of Ell's suitcase into the drawers.

Later, after a suitable dose of mint chocolate chip all around, Kristen went back to Jake's house and Ell went to her new room to reorganize. Though it was late when she finished and laid down to sleep, sleep was long in coming. The fight with Jake kept cycling through her mind. Normally, when Ell had trouble getting to sleep, she mentally did some math. Originally it had been the taking of advanced courses. More recently she had been working on her favorite math and physics problem, an attempt to describe how quantum entanglement could occur through another dimension.

One of the great mysteries of physics is how particles which are entangled somehow seem to be connected to one another even when they're far apart. Ell was trying to create her own math to describe how such entangled particles, despite being separated in the dimensions we're aware of, might actually be in direct contact with one another through a postulated additional dimension. Thus they could touch each other in this other dimension even though, in the dimensions we see, they were far apart. The problem was mind boggling and the mental effort usually wore her down and put her off to sleep.

This night however, her mind kept derailing off her dimensional math and back onto Jake. *And* what Jake had done, *and* how Ell *should've* responded.

This time it was almost morning before she finally

fell asleep.

***

Phil Zabrisk first encountered Ell on a brisk fall Saturday at the service academy physmed trials. It'd been cool in the morning, but an Indian Summer sun brought a beautiful breezy afternoon with brightly colored leaves fluttering everywhere. Phil's dad was currently stationed at Seymore Johnson Air Force Base in North Carolina and Phil happened to go to the Chapel Hill ROTC center for his physmed testing on the same date Ell went for hers.

His family had a long history of military service and it was his intention to extend that proud tradition. Many of his ancestors had served in the higher ranks of the nation's officer corps and it was the family's belief that breeding will show. Tales of Phil's forebears had inspired him and it was his intent to exceed their accomplishments. Most cadets are appointed to the service academies by members of Congress. Phil's Grandfather, Father and Uncle had easily pulled enough strings to ensure that Phil would get an appointment, assuming he passed the physmed testing and did even moderately well on the entrance exams. He'd done well enough on the entrance exams that his admission was practically guaranteed once he cleared physmed. Phil excelled at wrestling; talk even circulated about his chances for All-American status in college. No one had much concern that he might be physically disqualified.

Ell, on the other hand, had been a quandary for the Academies. She was underage and their lower age limit for admission was supposed to be inviolate. However, recruiters had been very excited about her math abilities.

Then they'd heard about her phenomenal scores on a reaction time test.

They'd offered to guarantee admission if she'd wait until she was of age but she'd refused. Then the honorable Senator Lloyd Danbridge of North Carolina, who'd put her up for admission, raised a stink. The Air Force Academy had finally agreed to make an exception in her case, as long as she kept her age a secret from other cadets. After all, she *would* be of age by the time she graduated and started full active duty. Nonetheless she had to pass the physmed testing like everyone else or she wouldn't be allowed in. Ell worried because one of the requirements was that she be able to run a mile in under seven minutes. Despite her superb athletic abilities in fast reaction time sports, Ell's endurance was *terrible*.

Pell and Phil worked very far apart as they went through the line doing their testing. While Phil stood in his shorts, being poked and prodded by the medicos, his mind wasn't really on what they were doing. Completely confident he would pass physmed, he was doing a little girl watching on the women who were also there to be tested. Ell was three places ahead of him in line.

He noticed her because he thought she had a fine looking body. She was above average in height and slender, but muscularly very well defined. He smirked to himself, thinking that she'd probably wasted a lot of effort getting herself in shape for this test in the vain hope that it'd help her get an appointment. Nonetheless, she looked good from behind and Phil surely appreciated the view. When she turned his way at one point he realized that her face had an elegant symmetry. *The girl's hot!* he thought to himself.

At one of the testing stations, a screen displayed the entire list of applicants snaking their way through and by counting up three names he was able to determine that she was "Donsaii, Ell." The examiners hadn't taken the testee's electronics away from them at that point so he simply queried his AI about her. With an unusual name like that she wasn't hard to find. A few seconds later his AI Chuck began whispering in his ear. "She doesn't have a very big presence on the public net. She grew up in Morehead City, on the North Carolina coast. Only child of a widowed mother. Father and grandfather owned a fishing boat that sank with both aboard. Mother currently works as a teacher in the winter, waitress in the summer. Went to public schools. Very good grades, played on several athletic teams, usually the star of the team. She is probably a very well qualified applicant."

With those genes she might make a good noncom, Phil thought to himself.

The next place Phil's mind went was even lower. He decided a small town girl, with great legs, whom he was never going to see again, made a perfect candidate for an onslaught of Zabrisk charm. He asked Chuck to look up her accomplishments on the net and focused on the fact that she'd been a pitcher on the State Championship softball team from her high school.

Later, when Phil happened to see the girls finishing their one mile run, he saw with surprise that, even though she looked muscular and physically fit, Donsaii came in dead last. He wondered if she'd even made it by the seven-minute maximum. As they wound through the interminable afternoon of strength, quickness, and reaction time testing and then got their blood drawn for genetic analysis, he saw her here and there and ran through a few lines in his head. He kept a close eye on her and, when they hit the showers, he hustled his so he could be out well before she was. He figured he'd have plenty of time—the women he'd known so far were pretty slow getting dressed and made-up.

However, despite hurrying, he almost missed her—she was walking out of the building when he left the changing room. He jogged a few steps to catch up and said, "Ell Donsaii?" She turned with a curious look on her face. *My God,* he thought, *she really is beautiful!* "Did you play softball for West Carteret? I saw your name ahead of mine on the lists in the test center."

She frowned.

Phil smiled, "A buddy of mine who's a softball fan went on and on about watching 'Ell Donsaii from Morehead City' play in the State championship. He said she was an incredible player and I just wondered if you were the same girl."

She broke open a big smile of full lips and straight white teeth when she replied, "Uh-huh, I was on the team," a crease developed between her eyebrows, "but I was just one of the players. Softball's a team effort you know."

Bingo, he thought to himself. *Nothing like a little stroke to go to a girl's head.* "Well that's not the way he told it. Weren't you the pitcher? *And* batted in a couple of runs? He made it seem like you were the only player on the team." he gave a sidelong glance at her cute pixie-like nose, "Or maybe he just couldn't take his eyes off such a great-looking girl?" She actually blushed! "No, really," he said with a little shrug, "Joe told me so many tales about your game that I really do think he was watching the way you played, not *just* watching you."

Despite her blush, her grin got even bigger and a little lopsided as she looked up at the tall, handsome Phil. He knew he had a big, blond, square jawed, muscular Viking kind of look.

"Are you trying to pick me up?" she grinned. Her green eyes flashed and she looked positively delighted. "No one's ever tried to pick me up before!"

Most kids Phil's age probably would have been embarrassed at having been caught out in a transparent attempt, but not Phil. It simply reinforced his opinion that she was a naive small town hick, ripe for plucking. He ducked his head and scuffed his toe, trying to look a little embarrassed. "Yeah, it's just that you're so pretty. I was hoping I could buy you a coffee."

She looked positively radiant. "Sure, that'd be fun. Want to walk down to Franklin Street? We could take in a little Tar Heel history."

"Sure," they turned and headed that way. He watched her out of the corner of his eye. She walked with an easy grace on legs that seemed impossibly long and slender for her height. Wavy, thick, reddish blond hair bounced silkily about her neck. *Wow, what a looker*, he thought to himself. *And, such a small town nerd*! His confidence grew. Surely he'd be able to sweep this one off her feet.

They stopped into` an old Seattle Coffee shop and sat at the counter. Phil drew her out—on the theory than nothing impresses a woman more than a good listener. She told him about the small high school she attended and shrugged off her athletic accomplishments as due to the small conference they competed in. Her mom "worked hard but wouldn't be able to send her to college" so a Service Academy education looked like a great deal to her. She "sure hoped" she'd get into one of them. He nodded through the recital, waiting impatiently while dusk slowly fell and pondering his chances for scoring. Realistically, he didn't think his chances were very good, having just met this small town girl, but who knows? A little fling in the big city, maybe?

~~~

Eventually it got fairly dark out. "Oh! Look it's gotten pretty dim out there. Can I walk you back to your car?"

Guilelessly, "Oh I can find it, no problem."

"Ah, but this is the big city. A beautiful girl like you shouldn't walk around alone after dark." Phil wondered if he'd laid it on too thick, but she didn't seem to notice.

"That's sweet. Sure."

They set off at a leisurely pace. He'd hoped her car'd be parked near some semi romantic location, so he became delighted when they neared a landmark. "Hey, that's the Old Well. Want to go make a wish?"

"Okay"

Soon he had her sitting beside him on the bench in front of the well, talking about the Old Well and telling him how she'd love to be able to afford to go to Carolina. He snuck a hand behind her and onto her shoulder. She turned and grinned lopsidedly, "Are you tryin' to get fresh?"

"I can't help myself, you've really affected me."

"Oh, you're sweet." She gave him a peck on the cheek. "But we'd better get going," she said, turning out from under his arm and bouncing to her feet.

"Aww." But he got up with her and they continued on their way to her car. She let him put his arm back
~~~

around her shoulder as they walked. He marveled at how great her firm hip felt as it occasionally bumped against his thigh. To his delight, her car was parked in a dimly lit corner of the lot. He let her open her door and then stepped in close for a kiss.

She turned her head aside. "Thanks for the coffee, but I don't know you well enough for this."

"Oh, come on. Just one little kiss."

She leaned back with a shy grin on her face and looked him in the eye, "Nope. Maybe we'll get to know each other better if we both get into the same academy?"

That reminded him that he was never going to see her again. He took a firmer grip on her shoulder and turned her toward him, leaning in harder. "Oh, *come* on."

"I said no!"

~~~

Ell felt her heart pounding and her world starting to slow down. Her gut clenched as she realized she was falling into her "fight or flight" zone. Something bad could easily happen!

~~~

Phil mistook her tone for intimidated fear and thought she was about to buckle. He exerted just a little bit more of the power that had won him so many wrestling matches, drawing her closer.

"Stop!" Her hand swung back, a little handbag in it.

He pulled slightly harder, leaning in for the kiss and laughing inside at the thought of being hit by a purse.

Right up to the moment it exploded against the side of his face.

Phil staggered back.

Though he never saw it coming, a second blast of agony exploded over him when she kicked him in the crotch.

To his dismay he found himself writhing on the ground, curled about his ravished groin, holding his face, unable to breath. Waves of agony pulsed slowly through him.

Dimly, he expected her to jump in her car and leave. Instead, she leaned down next to him saying, "Oh my God! Phil! I'm so sorry! You scared me! Oh! You look pretty bad." he heard her talking to her AI and realized she was calling for an *ambulance*! His first reaction was that *an ambulance* was ridiculous; he'd just been slapped in the face with a purse and kicked in the nuts! By a *girl*! He'd be fine.

Surely, he'd be fine?

But Phil's body was telling him differently. To his dismay, he felt like he really did need a doctor. He rolled to his side and threw up his coffee.

Phil was in so much pain he didn't consider the fact that the police would be interested in the events leading up to his injury. When the ambulance arrived, he tried, but couldn't stand up by himself. To his humiliation; they loaded him on a stretcher like a sack of potatoes.

Before the ambulance left for the hospital, the police had arrived and relieved him of his AI. Dimly he heard Ell telling them, "I'm so sorry. He *just* wanted a kiss. But then he wouldn't take 'no' for an answer! I am so, so, sorry. He just seemed to be *so* strong. I couldn't keep from getting frightened."

"So what happened then?"

"I hit him with my purse."

"You hit him with your purse!?" The voice was bemused. "And that laid him out like this?"

"Well I hit him *really* hard. I didn't intend to, I overreacted. Then when he stepped back, I kicked him in the crotch. I *really* shouldn't have done that 'cause he'd already let go. But he was so strong—I was afraid that he might come after me again."

"You hit him with your purse and you kicked him in the nuts?" The voice said dryly, "Then you called him an ambulance!?" Phil could hear the smirk in the man's voice.

"Well, I'd kicked him really hard and he seemed to be having trouble breathing and then he threw up." She paused, then said plaintively, "Really, I think he's a nice guy who just got a little out of control."

"A nice guy who was a 'little out of control'? I can't wait to download the records on this!"

Phil felt even sicker inside as the doors of the ambulance closed. When the police downloaded the audio-visual records from his and Ell's AIs, he was going to look pretty bad. With a sinking feeling, he considered the possibility that this event might even keep him out of an academy. He didn't consider the fact that an assault or attempted rape conviction might have worse ramifications than being dropped off the academy admission lists.

~~~

Zabrisk spent hours in the Emergency department where they told him that Donsaii's "purse" had broken the bony zygomatic arch in his cheek, but that the fracture wasn't far enough out of place to require surgery. They also told him that there was significant hemorrhage in his scrotum, but that there wasn't really any treatment for that. Ice and pain medication would
~~~

be his friends for the next 72 hours.

"Officer?" he heard his doctor say, after stepping outside the curtain of his cubicle. "What's the story on how this guy got hurt?"

"Girl hit him with her purse doc." There was a snigger in the policeman's voice.

"Come on! Did she have a brick in it?"

"Not near as we can tell. This here's the purse. Couldn't even fit a brick inside an itty bitty thing like that."

"This girl on steroids or what?"

"Honest, doc, she's five foot eight, maybe five nine, slender, maybe a hundred twenty or thirty pounds. All girl. Really, really cute."

"Come on! This guy's what, 220, and in shape? Sure she didn't drug him, then run over him with a car?"

"Doc, the whole deal's recorded on their AIs. He tries to kiss her, she says 'No'. He tries again, she hits him with her purse. Boom! She kick him inna nuts. Boom! He falls down, he pukes, he gasps for breath… I shit you not."

Even though he'd lived through it, the whole story sounded implausible to Phil as well. How *could* this have happened?

Before he left the ER, the policeman came in to talk to him with a smirk on his face. "Next time a lady says 'No' Zabrisk, I trust you'll respect her wishes?"

"Yes sir." he was sullen inside, but all respect on the outside. "Nothing like this will *ever* happen again sir." He *had* to get this guy on his side. Phil desperately tried to think of extenuating circumstances that might diminish any charges she'd made.

"Well, you're a very lucky boy—despite my strong encouragement that she do so, she's not pressing charges." He handed Chuck back to him. Phil tried to put the AI's headset back on, but Chuck's frame was too bent to fit! Phil settled for hanging the frame over the belt pack.

"I'd encourage you to look at the record your AI made of the evening's events." The policeman's eyebrows waggled, "You'll be surprised."

At that point, Phil couldn't imagine what could be surprising about the record, other than the fact that it documented his two hundred twenty five pound ass getting kicked by a twig of a girl. However, he was determined to act like a citizen. "Yes sir." Inside, he was greatly relieved about the lack of charges against him; at least his chances of an academy appointment should remain intact. Briefly, he was a grateful to her. But as he got up off the bed and found out just how agonizing the next few days were going to be, a wave of anger flowed back over him.

~~~

Phil rode home with a bag of ice in his crotch, glad for a moment that the car's AI meant he didn't actually have to drive. Even though the AI drove, the ride was another crappy experience with each bump and corner eliciting stabs of agony from his crotch and face. He groaned up the steps to the house, commiserating with himself, then found to his dismay that his folks were waiting up to find out how he thought he'd done at the Physmed testing! *For God's sake how could they worry about that. I'm in incredible physical condition.*

"Hey Phil, how'd it go... Jeez, what happened to you?!"

He leaned up against the doorframe, standing as straight as he could. Briefly, he considered trying to tell
~~~

the truth. *Nah...* "It went good, but I slipped in the showers after the testing and blasted my face into a shower handle. Can you believe it?!" He started up the stairs to his room.

"Why are you limping?"

"I did the splits when I fell. Pulled my groin. I'll be okay—eventually. I'm hittin' the rack, okay?" He struggled on up to his room where he was astonished to see his face in the mirror. He was black and blue from his hairline to the jaw on the left side. And that said nothing of the puffy swelling that distorted the shape of his head. When he got his pants down, his nuts were black and blue, and three times as big as they normally were. The way they felt, it hardly surprised him.

He crashed onto the bed and straightened Chuck's frame enough to get the headset back on his head. He asked Chuck to pull up the record of the bitch's attack and display it for him on his HUD. Phil looked up into the screens hanging over his eyes and saw Ell's face projected back in front of him, looking just like she had out there by her car. To his surprise, he noticed she actually did look pretty frightened as he tried to pull her closer. Why would a little kiss frighten her? Her right hand with the little leather purse in it swung backward into the view from the camera as she wound up. Then it disappeared. Static streaked the screens as the electronics of his HUD dealt with the blow in their own way. The world turned topsy-turvy and bobbled, evidently as he'd staggered back. His head had dropped some and Chuck's frame was tilted on his head so the screens showed Ell's legs at an oblique angle. He thought once again about how nice they looked. One leg swung back and then blurred toward him. The view slammed drunkenly into the ground to show nothing but pavement. But the audio record rolled on. For a few seconds Ell said "Ohmygodohmygodohmygod" then, just like he remembered, she apologized to him.

Next she had her AI contact 911 and asked for an ambulance.

He still couldn't believe what he'd just seen. "Chuck, run that back and give me a frame by frame for a couple seconds before she hit me." It didn't look like she was doing anything to prepare her purse before she hit him. Though the purse itself was out of Chuck's field of view, her shoulders didn't move like she was doing anything with her hands and she certainly didn't talk to her AI. When the purse came into view it didn't look bulky, as if she had a rock or anything in it. Just a small leather purse, a little bigger than her hand. At its full backswing, he saw her fingers disappear behind it. It wasn't like she was using it for extra weight—she was using it to protect her hand, like a boxing glove!

There were only two frames in the video once her hand started to move toward his head and they were extremely blurred by motion artifact. Phil lay there in amazement, pondering what he'd just witnessed. He tried having Chuck make a record of him swinging his hands as fast as he could—he couldn't swing his hand fast enough to generate that much blur! How did she *do* that?

Phil drifted off to sleep still pondering the question.

~~~

Over the next couple of days, he wondered occasionally about what had happened, and then tried to forget it.

He'd never see the girl again anyway.
~~~

***

For her part Ell felt horrified. She knew that when something stimulated her fight or flight reaction, she consistently moved into what she now referred to as “the zone." It had happened with the man who had been going to rape her mother. It had happened with Jake when he tried to slap her. Both times someone had been badly hurt. She desperately wanted to get better control of herself when she was in her zone.

A milder version occurred sometimes during games but she’d never hurt anyone when she was playing sports. She’d once broken a volleyball with a hard spike, but everyone just assumed the ball’d been worn out or flawed. She had such great control in the kind of mild zone she got into playing sports that she didn’t have to worry that she might spike a ball into someone’s face. Even though she didn’t worry about hurting anyone playing sports, she’d learned to pull her spikes so that ball speed and bounce height after those spikes didn’t spook people. Pitching softball she worked hard to stay almost completely out of the zone.

She’d decided on that after a couple of pitches that’d really hurt the catcher’s hand… right through the mitt.

She thought what happened with her had to be the same as that eerie effect of being in the zone other athletes sometimes experience fleetingly. Most athletes *want* it to happen all the time. Everything seems to decelerate so it moves in slow motion.

When they got in the zone, those athletes felt like their coordination became almost supernatural.

Exactly the way Ell felt when it happened to her.

Most athletes have been in a zone on occasion.

You're playing someone that usually beats you. Then suddenly things slow down so that you have what seems like minutes to line up and execute.

In the zone you simply destroy your previously dominating opponent. For Ell, her normal quickness became exceptional speed; speed *so* phenomenal that other people usually just didn't believe what they'd seen. She didn't want to be thought a freak, so she worked hard to slow down when she felt the zone coming on. But when she was truly frightened, she *couldn't* slow it down completely.

No more than she could still her own beating heart.

She knew her struggle with Zabrisk had been recorded on both of their AIs and she was beside herself worrying that the police would review the record carefully enough to recognize that something bizarrely abnormal had happened.

Ell agonized over it the entire ride home but to her great relief the car's AI delivered her back to Morehead City where she found her Gram waiting for her without any messages from the police. None came over the next few days either, so Ell gradually relaxed.

***

Tucson was hot. Everyone said so. Jamal agreed it was hot, though not when compared to his homeland. Amazing to him was the profligate use of air conditioning. Air conditioning that, to him, rendered the indoors downright chilly. He lived in a small apartment in a complex just off of Speedway, only a few blocks from his classes at the University of Arizona. He studied Civil Engineering.

Engineering wasn't his best subject by any means. Instead, it was the subject that his masters believed held the most promise for use in their war against America.

Jamal, when he thought about it, felt both surprise and respect for his masters' remarkable patience in deploying him against their enemy. If there were other young men, studying as he was for a future strike against the Americans, he'd never to his knowledge met one. If there was a definite plan for Jamal's own strike, he hadn't been made aware of it. If a time for his strike had been set, that time had been hidden from him.

Sometimes Jamal almost forgot that he stood ready.

A weapon in the arsenal of justice against America. This became especially easy to forget after he had spent a couple of years at the University. Though he didn't drink or party with his classmates, he found that many of them had become good friends. He struggled in some classes and joined study groups. They drank coffee and joked together in ways that he, at first, couldn't comprehend. But later Jamal grew to enjoy their camaraderie. Because there were many international students at the University, Jamal tended to assume that his friends were also from other countries.

Jamal was stunned when he found that Inad, whom Jamal had believed to be on a student visa from Jordan, proved to be a second generation American and fiercely proud of his family's adopted country. Inad produced diatribes against American policy in the student e-paper. Jamal asked him one day, "Inad, how can you be so critical of this country, yet say you are so proud of it?"

"Because, my dim bulb, of just that." Inad said, sipping at his coffee. They sat in a small, overly cooled café on the edge of campus. "Because even I, a student, am *allowed* to tell people through my column, what is wrong with this country so that it might be made better. My father had to *flee* Jordan after he criticized the government. Even if I hadn't been accepted as a columnist by the student e-news I could *still* publish on the internet without being arrested—I just wouldn't have as many readers."

"But Inad, nothing changes. Your columns fall on deaf ears. No one cares. No one believes!"

"Ah, my simple friend, that's not true. Much does not change. My columns are not read or understood by most. Few care or believe. But! Some change occurs, occasionally someone listens, a few *do* believe. And, my friend, it's *my* responsibility to convince them. To write so powerfully that they *must* take heed. If my argument's so weak that no one's swayed, then that's my fault, not theirs, eh?"

Jamal said nothing for a moment, then grinned, "Well then, it *is* your fault. As far as I can tell, no one *has* been swayed!"

Inad looked startled. Then a wry grin crossed his face and he struck his friend on the shoulder. "Jamal, I think you just tried to say something funny! Have you been partaking of the evils of repartee?"

Chapter Two

Phil wasn't looking forward to his Doolie year at the Academy, but excitement coursed through him as they were hustled through the induction. They got their hair buzzed short and had their uniform fittings. Head molds were taken to fit their military AIs. They got some basic instruction in military and cadet rank, and then were shown to dorm rooms. Phil ogled the female doolies. Some were pretty cute, some were nothing to write home about, but it was certainly better than all guys. The upperclassmen that shepherded them around were polite and nothing like the hell on wheels he'd been expecting from his Dad's stories of the old days. They taught the doolies the rudiments of marching and how their uniforms were supposed to be kept up.

His roommate disabused him of the notion that things might be getting softer at the Academy. "Sheeit, man. They've toughened up, not softened, the past ten, twenty years. There was some time a few decades back, probably after your dad was here, when they tried to civilize the Academy experience and stop the humiliation and harassment, but not any more." His roommate's brother'd just graduated and filled him in. "The first couple of days they go easy because it's too hard to process us if we're scared shitless." Phil lay down to sleep thinking his roommate was full of crap.

The next morning a klaxon blasted them out of bed at 0500 and the upperclassmen who'd been politely shepherding them around slammed their doors open. Unsmilingly, they told the doolies to get into their athletic gear and herded them out onto the parade ground. The eastern Colorado sky was just turning a delicate pink as they were lined up in a formation with different files in it than they'd been in the day before.

The upperclassmen who'd been working with them so far formed up with great military precision and silently marched away to a distant drumbeat. Phil was standing there gawking and wondering what the hell was happening. He started admiring the babe just ahead of him in the file to his left. Strawberry blond hair, great looking legs—then she looked to the right and he saw her face in profile. *Holy shit! It's that bitch, Donsaii!*

Surprise and goose bumps washed over him. He simply could *not* believe she was here. He'd been absolutely convinced that there was no way she had what it took to get in. Even if she did squeak in, *surely* it would have been to one of the other academies.

Anger and rage boiled through him. His fury kept him from noticing as a new set of upperclassmen marched up and took their place at the front of their formation. Then there was a loud pop off over near the drummer and a sputtering trail arced through the sky. The firework detonated high over the parade ground and the new upperclassmen shouldered back through the doolies' ranks to begin screaming at their charges. The doolies' posture, their bearing, the way their t-shirts were tucked into their shorts, the way their shoes were tied, and the way they were formed up. All of this was grist for the upperclassmen's dismay at having "been saddled with such worthless scum."

Phil snapped to attention as soon as it started, so for a minute or so they ignored him. Delight coursed through him when a short squatty upperclasswoman stopped on Ell's right front quarter and leaned up into her face, bellowing so loudly that the Cadet's face turned red and spittle flew from her lips. Ell jerked up into better posture, head back, chin tucked in, and hands rigidly at her side.

Suddenly the upperclasswoman caught a view of Phil's grin out of the corner of her eye. She wheeled and stalked a pace back to lean into his face, a dangerous and loathing look in her eye. "And *you*, smack. Just what are you *smirkin'* about, huh?" She no longer screamed at the top of her lungs, but seemed all the more menacing for her low tone. "You think it's funny that one of your classmates is in a world of shit? You think you're better than her?"

She paused. "I'M TALKIN' TO YOU SMACK!" She exploded.

"Uh, n-n-no..."

"NO! No, what?"

"Uh, No sir, I mean Ma'am."

"You'd better not '*sir'* me squat!"

"No Ma'am."

"Now one thing you, *and* the rest of the squatwads around you that can hear me, better learn, and learn fast, is that if somethin' causes one of your classmates pain, it *causes you* pain. You DO NOT laugh 'cause one of your classmates is in trouble. You do *everything* in your power to help your classmates stay out of trouble, and to get them *out* of trouble if they're in it. GOT ME?"

"Yes Ma'am."

"CAN'T HEAR YOU!"

"YES MA'AM."

"Why the hell is your chin stickin' way the hell out there? You tryin' to keep the rain off your shoes or is it just that no one ever taught you how to stand at attention?" She criticized Phil's posture a few minutes longer, then took on the doolie to his right.

The screaming went on for what seemed like forever but probably was no more than fifteen minutes, then another firework popped off and the upperclassmen filed back out of their formation to stand at the front. The short female cadet who'd been in Phil's face earlier took two steps towards them and bellowed, "Listen up scuzzbuckets! I'm Cadet Captain Andrews and I have the unfortunate task of trying to whip G squadron, that's your squadron of dipweeds, into some kind of military shape. First thing we're gonna do is go for a little mornin' run to whet your appetites and start getting' you lardbuckets up to minimal physical specs. To do this we're divvyin' up into five squads of twenty. Each squad is headin' out for a short little run with its cadet lieutenant and sergeants. We'll all meet back here to march in for breakfast. G Squadron, Ten-Hut!" This last seemed superfluous since they were already straining at attention. "Squad leaders break 'em out."

The upperclassmen milled around and a pimply faced redhead strode up to stand between the front of the column Phil was in and the front of the column to their left. Then he bellowed at a volume Phil wouldn't have believed possible for such a dweeby looking guy, "You tew columns! You ahr C squad. Ah'm Caydet Lieutenant Johnson and the two Caydet Sergeants behind me ahr Smith and Zymonds. Yoah asses are ours! Let's see if you miserable excuses can march off the parade grounds. Forward—Harch!"

Amazing! A southern accent thicker than Phil'd ever heard, even back in North Carolina?

Of course, despite their brief instruction in marching over the past few days, the doolies started off higgledy-piggledy. Phil expected Johnson to scream at them, but instead he started bellowing time. "Layft, layft, laaayft-rayht-layft. Yer other layft Donsaii, fer chrys sake! Layft, layft, layft-raight-layft. Layft turn... Harch!" They blew the turn too, but Johnson and the two sergeants bellowed and shoved to get them back into line. At least into a good enough formation to get off the parade grounds. "Column... Halt!" They came to a staggered stop.

"Hoolllly sheeit! Thet has to be the worst excuse for a marching foahmation Ah have evah seen. Smith! Zymonds! Do you think we'll ever be able to whip their sorry asses into shape?"

"No, sir!" They bellowed in unison.

The southern accent disappeared, "Well, right now they're here to run, not march. Forward... March! On the double... Ho! Left, left, left, left."

The squad headed out between some athletic fields at an easy jog. Though he didn't let it show on his face, Phil was sneering inside at the thought that running with Johnson was going to give *him* any exercise. Phil was in great shape, much better shape than *that* dweeby guy. Or so Phil thought. Pretty soon, the mile-high altitude started to tell and Phil's breathing started coming a little harder. After a while, it came a *lot* harder. Before he really had a chance to worry about his own stamina though, he noticed gaps developing in their formation where some of the weaker Dools were having a hard time keeping up. Smith and Zymonds were right there on the gaps, bawling at the slackers.

The yelling amazed Phil, He sure didn't have the breath left to yell at anyone!

"You!" Zymonds was bellowing in his ear. She looked up at the name on Phil's t-shirt, "Zabrisk! Help your classmate!" She waved a hand at the doolie in front of Phil who was falling back. "Like this!" She grabbed the cadet's hand and pulled it up onto her shoulder, running a few steps in tandem with her, towing her along. "Now you, Zabrisk!"

Furious, Phil pulled up beside the cadet and dragged her limp hand up onto his shoulder. *Why do I have to pick up this bitch's slack?* He saw up ahead that Donsaii was being pulled along by another of the stronger doolies. It surprised him because she *looked* more physically fit than any of the other women. Apparently she was weaker than she looked.

The squad leaders kept them going till they all felt like they were dying.

Then they kept them going till they all wished they'd already died.

The stronger ones were dying just as much as the weak 'cause the strong ones were hauling the weaker Dools along till they were on their last legs as well. Ell and one of the softer looking guys finished the run practically being carried by doolies on either side of them. When the cadet sergeants finally called a halt, a couple of the doolies fell to their knees, but Johnson, Smith and Zymonds were right there in their faces yelling at them to get up and walk it out.

Phil saw Donsaii bend over, grab her knees and puke. That brought a weak grin to his face. Unfortunately, Cadet Captain Andrews chose that moment to hove into view. "What are *you* grinnin' about" she looked down at his nametag, "Zabrisk?

Maybe you're hopin' to run a little farther? I *know* you're not laughin' at one of your classmates!"

"No Ma'am."

"Stand at attention when you speak to me!"

"Yes Ma'am."

"Now, don't smirk, help your classmates who're in trouble walk around. You don't want them to cramp up do you?"

"No Ma'am."

"You smacks! Listen up! This chain's only as strong as its weakest squat! Got that?"

A weak chorus, "Yes Ma'am."

"What?!"

Stronger, "Yes Ma'am."

"That means, if you're a weak link, you better try harder. If you're a strong link, you better help those weak links hold up their ends! Got it?"

"Yes Ma'am."

"You weak links, you'd *better* get in shape! If you can't run a six minute mile by the end of the summer you're outta here. Got that too?"

~~~

"Yes Ma'am." They chorused again. Ell, dispiritedly, worrying because her terrible endurance made just the thought of running a mile painful. The possibility that she might get drummed out of the Academy if she couldn't run a mile under six minutes, after enduring this kind of torture all summer, horrified her.

~~~

They started marching back toward the parade ground. The doolie in front of Phil started staggering, so he grabbed her and threw her arm over his shoulder.

They were doing okay but then Ell just fell over, right in front of them.

Phil stepped over her.

"Column… Halt. What the HELL 're you doin' squat?" it was Zymonds, in Phil's face.

"Ma'am, I'm helping this cadet, Ma'am."

"What about the one you just stepped over, smack?"

"Ma'am, I… I thought someone *else* would help her, Ma'am." He couldn't tell Zymonds that *Hell* would freeze over before he helped that particular classmate. Out of the corner of his eye he could see that someone had bent over and was trying to bring Ell around. She seemed to be out cold though. Eventually they marched back up to the parade ground and then the squadron marched into the cafeteria.

Ell was still out there with Cadet Sergeant Smith.

Smith dragged Ell in a few minutes later and sat her in the empty chair across from Phil.

Ell didn't look too much worse for the wear and, as soon as she sat down, her eyes widened to see Phil sitting there. Astonishment coursed over him as she gave him a crooked smile and a one finger wave—as if he were some kind of long lost friend! Breakfast was eaten at attention, so no words passed between them. In fact, the whole morning passed with no words spoken amongst the doolies. They marched, they ran, they attended a class on military ethics, they marched and then they got a little break out under the trees before they marched back in to lunch.

"Hey, Phil, how're you doin'?" Ell just flopped down and started talking to him like they were old buddies! He guessed they might know each other better than any other two members of their squad, or maybe the entire squadron. It just didn't seem to him like they knew each other in a way that'd be conducive to a pleasant greeting.

When he didn't answer, just sat there with his back to a little pine tree staring at her, she said, "Hey, you still pissed? I'm really, really sorry about what happened back there in Chapel Hill. You just scared me, and when my adrenalin gets pumpin' funny things happen."

At the time he had *some* idea just what kind of things could happen when her adrenalin got pumping, but he didn't understand what he knew. In any case, it became evident that she held no grudge over his familiarities on that day last fall. Phil kinda wished the same were true for him.

***

As their basic training progressed, Phil's excellent physical conditioning stood him in good stead. Even though being in shape for wrestling wasn't quite the right kind of conditioning for the type of high altitude endurance running and calisthenics they were going through, his conditioning so far outstripped most of the other doolies that he wasn't under a great deal of strain. Of course, there were some cross country runners and other endurance athletes who felt it even less than he did, but the biggest pain for him was having to help drag along the doolies who *were* out of shape. Some of them quit the Academy rather than endure the daily agony. With the biggest anchors gone, the whole squad's speed picked up, but never to a level that really stressed Phil.

On the other hand, Ell's struggles with the endurance parts of their conditioning were legendary. Passing out on that first run indicated the problem. Though she never went out cold again, she did throw up almost every time they did a run. Annoyingly, though she herself struggled, she kept trying to help those around her; always a "buck up, there" comment for those who were dying around her. Hell, she'd be looking like death's own sister and she'd still stagger over to try to help another doolie!

Phil found it frustrating because her charity used up her reserves faster. Then *she* needed help sooner. She had to be helped by her classmates on any run of a mile or more.

The sergeant would yell at her for being so weak and Phil would smirk inside. But then the upperclassmen would rain shit on Phil because *he* wasn't trying to help the other doolies like she was; obviously, he had more reserves than she did.

So, she made him look bad. Their relationship sat in the toilet and sank.

Ell didn't seem to understand that he hated her guts. She frequently complimented him for helping out the weak dipwads in their squad—which *did* make him feel good. But the warm feeling from the compliment washed over him without reflecting back on her.

No one else seemed to hate her though. It was easy to see why—amazingly good looking young woman, always trying unselfishly to help the others.

Even when she was in worse shape than they were.

Hard to hate.

Ell's poor scores on endurance tests dragged the squad down. But, though Phil's blind spot meant that he hardly noticed it, her high scores on tests requiring speed or coordination brought the squad up. Rather than simply riding her, the upperclassmen actually seemed to be trying to help her!

~~~

For her part, Ell worried a lot. Despite all the exercise, her endurance didn't seem to improve. Throwing up every day seemed to be sucking the life out of her, to say nothing of the physical exhaustion that'd made her puke in the first place. Other doolies were dropping out of the Academy, and every day during their runs the dropouts' example led her to think of giving up herself. But she *couldn't* return home with her tail between her legs. She couldn't *stand* the thought of seeing that knowing smirk on Jake's face. So, day after day, she suffered the agony of the training. She suffered the embarrassment of being dragged the last part of any endurance endeavor by her classmates. When her classmates spoke quietly outside her hearing she worried that they were talking about her and her inadequacy. Her greatest fear was that there were some other minimum physical standards in addition to the six-minute mile that she'd have difficulty measuring up to by the end of the summer. She dreaded the possibility that that they'd wash her out *despite* all this agonizing effort.

~~~

Phil couldn't reconcile the wimp chick with no staying power with the woman who'd beat the crap out of him one night back home. However, the second thing Basic began to reveal about her, even to Phil, was her surprising speed. Her performance at the beginning of the obstacle course seemed freakish. She'd start *way* faster than anyone else could. Climbing, jumping, swinging, leaping over stuff—Ell *was* the best in the squad, significantly quicker than any of the guys even. She performed some amazing feats—at the start of the course.

No one, not even any of the guys could stay even close behind her in the first half of the route. But the obstacle course was long. By the end, she'd be dragging. A run that started out like it'd break records finished with her staggering across the finish line—with a time that actually pulled the squadron's average down. When Zymonds told her to start slower, it just made things worse! She still dragged badly by the end and, without the lead provided by her jackrabbit start, her time on the course was even worse.

~~~

A few weeks into Basic, a run took them out into the woods where they took a break in the shade for lunch. After lunch they had a short break while waiting for an instructor who was supposed to give them a survival lecture. It was hot and a lot of the guys took off their shirts, Phil among them. Ell's eyebrows ascended, *the guy was built like a Greek God!* Wide shoulders, narrow waist, ripped abs, huge arms, his physique was *amazing*. She found it surprisingly hard to take her eyes off him.

Then Phil got into a hand-slapping contest with Jason, another doolie who'd also been recruited for the wrestling team. It was the quickness competition where you put your hands out, palms up. Your opponent put his hands over yours, palms down. Then you tried to flip your hands out, over and down to slap your opponent on the backs of his hands. Phil'd always been very quick
~~~

at it but, to his surprise, Jason almost held his own with him.

Ell'd been covertly studying Phil's amazing musculature, so was watching them play the game. She wondered if she could break through the distance Phil always kept between the two of them by joining in something he enjoyed. She walked over to them and said, "Can I try?"

Phil just ignored her but Jason said, "Sure cuteness." Ell stepped forward with her trademark crooked smile and then noticed that everyone's attention had suddenly focused on her. The girls rarely challenged the guys on physical stuff and Jason was a real stud, so her act had grabbed the squad's attention.

Ell felt kinda pissed about being called "cuteness." In addition, the spotlight of everyone's attention gave her a little stage fright. She felt her heart beat start to throb. Realizing she was slipping into the zone, Ell took a couple deep breaths and shook out her hands, trying to damp it down. She reminded herself not to go too fast.

Ell was finding to her relief that, with some of the intense work she'd been doing on it, she was developing better and better control of when and how far she went into the zone. However, she *did* kinda want to put Jason in his place so she didn't try to come completely out of it this time.

"I'm usually pretty good at reaction time stuff," she said nervously, putting her hands over Jason's. Inwardly Phil sneered because Jason was *very* good. Phil felt certain Jason would put some serious hurt on her. Then Jason flipped to strike.

Donsaii's hands were gone! The first time Jason flipped and no contact! Phil blinked.

Jason said, "Oooohh, got *lucky*."

Well, Phil thought, *after all, there is some luck involved in not getting smacked, especially the first time you play. Part of winning is guessing when your opponent's going to flip and actually starting your withdrawal before he moves. It'd take a lotta luck against someone as good as Jason, but it could happen.*

Real lucky, Phil thought to himself. But it won't last.

Ell put her hands back out, palms up and Jason put his on top. Her pulse sounded as a slow throb in her ears and she realized that she'd slipped much deeper into the zone than she wanted. She knew she'd jerked her hands away too fast when they were on top, but hoped no one had noticed. *Slow down!* She reminded herself.

So, at a pace that felt slow, she pulled her hands out from under his and slid them smoothly out and around to come down on the backs of his hands.

She realized—from the fact that his hands hadn't even *started* moving when hers were coming down—that she was still moving way too fast! *No!*

She tried to slow even more in the last milliseconds but it was too late.

Her hands smacked his.

The dual impacts sounded like a gunshot! The palms of her hands stung badly and she wondered what it would feel like on the more sensitive backs of Jason's hands. Ell danced around with her fingers in her mouth, mumbling, "Sorry, sorry, too hard, too hard."

Jason's hands flew downward with the force of the blow and his eyes widened as he realized just *how badly* he'd been beaten.

~~~
~~~

When Jason put his trembling hands back out, the backs of his hands were scarlet! Phil saw with amazement that Jason's eyes were watering! Ell asked, "Are you really okay to go again? I *really* am sorry."

Jason just nodded, an astonished and apprehensive look on his face.

Phil watched with wide eyes. She didn't hit him hard again, but she whacked him over and over with ease, maybe twenty—thirty times. Then she seemed to realize how people were gawping and suddenly slowed down. *Way* down from the blurs her hands had been before. Jason finally managed a pull away. However, before he got to try slapping her again, the squad was called to form up for the lecture.

Over the next few weeks, other people would occasionally try to get her to hand-slap, but she always had an excuse and, if it happened, Phil never saw it. He thought of challenging her himself, but didn't. He told himself that it was because he couldn't stand her, but really, deep inside… he knew he didn't stand a *chance* against her.

~~~

They had some self-defense/combat sessions in Basic. They were aimed at developing self-confidence and aggression as well as teaching future warriors how to fight. Self-defense dealt with what to do if attacked. If attacked by a bigger, or by a smaller assailant. If attacked by an assailant with a knife. If assailed with a gun from afar they were to seek cover or submit. If threatened with a pistol from very close, and you didn't think submitting would save your life, you might try to disarm by striking or twisting the weapon in the direction that flexes the attacker's wrist and relaxes the
~~~

fingers. Such a move, by loosening the fingers, could prevent the trigger's being pulled. Multiple different techniques were taught, based in different fighting styles, many of them, in common parlance, "fighting dirty." But *when your life is on the line...*

For some aggressiveness sessions they squared off in marked circles called pits, wearing cushioned headgear and swinging pugil sticks. The sticks were about four and a half feet long with heavy pads at their ends. Of course, Phil thrived at it. His wrestling physique, conditioning, speed, and combative tendencies stood him well. Sergeant Mason, their large black instructor, took one look at Phil and used him for a demonstration bout. Phil and Mason moved through some of the strikes and counters in slow motion and finally went through a very brief bout where Phil tried to break through Mason's defenses without success. The sergeant then paired off same sex cadets of approximately equal size and they took turns in the pits while the sergeant bellowed directions.

Most of the matches were real flails. At that altitude, after a preliminary run out and around the fields, swinging those big sticks while someone else tried to pound you wore a body out in a hurry. Phil'd been paired with Jason, the other guy who'd done some wrestling, because Jason was almost a physical match. Jason busted him a couple of good ones but Phil knocked him out of the circle without too much trouble. They took a tongue-lashing from the instructor for their tendency to wrestle with the sticks instead of striking with them. But they could tell Sergeant Mason wasn't really all that upset.

Phil really didn't take too much interest in the other matches until the first time Ell got in the circle—that contest held his rapt attention!

Ell had been paired off with a woman named Joy Denson. Joy had a couple of inches on Ell. Thinking about his parking lot encounter, Phil found himself expecting Joy to get crushed. However, they fought like a couple of ladies at tea. Tap, tap, tap with their sticks, no single swing hard enough that the other woman couldn't catch it on her staff with plenty of time. Sergeant Mason purpled up, looking as if he were about to explode. "You *girls* knitting out here?"

They stopped, "No, sir!" In unison no less.

"Well those sticks aren't clickin' together any harder'n my old grandma's needles! Denson, you afraid you might hurt Cadet Donsaii?"

"No sir!"

"You ladies think, when lives are on the line, that kind of effort'll be good enough?"

In unison again, "No, sir!"

"Well then, *attack*, for god's sake, *attack*!"

Donsaii and Denson turned back toward one another. Denson, Phil gave her credit, really waded in. She swung her pugil stick, hard as she could, fast as she could and managed to look like her life might actually depend on it. *But she didn't touch Ell.*

Most of the other cadets didn't seem to notice what was happening in the pit, but it sent a chill up Phil's spine. Denson didn't even rap her on the knuckles. Every swing Denson made struck nothing but wood. Donsaii's staff magically interposed itself over and over and over and over... Most of the other cadets thought Denson was wailing on her, and in a sense she was... but not even an accidental whack struck home amidst all of Denson's fury.

Mason bellowed again, "You there! Stop! Donsaii!"

"Yes sir!"

"You ever hear that the best defense is a good offense?"

"Yes sir!"

"You think you might someday take a *poke* at Denson, or you too afraid she might actually land a blow?"

"Yes sir... I mean, No sir!"

"Let's try it again, ladies." A sneer dripped from the word "ladies." They turned to face each other and Mason roared, "Begin!"

More of the same ensued. Denson flailing away, Donsaii catching every blow. Mason bellowed again and Ell started taking an occasional whack. Phil's hair prickled on his neck. Every stroke she took hit Denson somewhere. Nary a one of them would have whisked a flake of dandruff off Denson's shoulder, but every one struck skin somewhere.

"Donsaii!"

They halted again, "Yes sir!"

"That was pitiful! My old gramma would do more harm with her aforementioned knittin' needles for Chrissake! Denson, outta the pit." The Sarge took Denson's staff and stepped menacingly into the pit across from Donsaii. "Donsaii!"

"Yes sir!"

"Hit me with that stick!" He held Denson's staff in the approved defensive position.

"Sir?"

"Hit me with that goddamn stick! I see you're afraid Denson might break—do I look tough enough to take a lickin'?"

"Yes sir!"

"Well. Don't just stand there, take a swing at me!"

"No sir! Striking a superior officer is a court martial offense, sir!"

"Aw fer Chrissake, we got ourselves a barracks lawyer? I'm a Sergeant, not an officer. *You* outrank me! You shouldn't even be 'sirring' me. Here I'll take off my insignia and tell you that if I *order* you to strike me in the course of training that it ain't no 'courts martial offense,' okay?" He stripped his insignia off its Velcro patch and tossed it aside.

"Yes sir!" Ell took a swing at him. A looping, roundhouse, poofter that Mason, dropping one end of his staff, easily blocked by grabbing the cushioned tip with the palm of his hand.

"My GOD that was pitiful!" Ell drooped while Mason berated her for her lack of aggression, finishing with, "If you don't get up the gumption to hit me a decent whack you'll be givin' me ten laps, ya delicate little puke!"

Ell lifted her staff, staring at Mason like a deer in the headlights.

Though Phil didn't understand what was going through her mind, Ell was already tired, even though it hadn't taken much exertion to block the strikes aimed at her so far. Ten laps in addition though, that would *exhaust* her.

"Sir?" she said.

"Hit me goddammit!" Ell took a couple of medium speed swings that Mason also blocked easily. "Come on, Attack! Don't stop. Do, not, stop!" She slipped a few blows past his stick, but whacked him with the same light glancing blows she'd used on Denson. "Donsaii?!"

"Yes sir!" She kept up her attack but still, you could tell, none of those blows would really have hurt anyone.

"May I have your permission to attack you? You see it's also a courts martial offense for me to strike you without your consent."

"Yes sir!" Phil didn't see it happen, but Ell's insignia patch flew over to land next to Mason's.

Mason started swinging at Ell. But just like with Denson, she blocked every blow perfectly. The whole time Mason screamed at her to attack him. "If you don't hit me a good hard whack I'm gonna wail away till your arms are dyin'. You'll miss a block and you'll get hurt... Who's it gonna be, you or me? Hit me so's I can feel it! Who's it gonna be, you or me?" Mason panted and grunted through this last and Phil could see Mason's swings getting harder and harder, then confusion crossing his face as he repeatedly failed to connect. Blow after blow, swung harder and harder, came down on her staff. They sounded like rifle shots! He was big, and strong, and quick. Phil doubted that Mason had *ever* failed to connect with them the first few blows when he tried this maneuver with timid cadets in the past.

~~~

Now Ell felt exhaustion coming on. She'd been in the pit for quite a while now and even just blocking the blows coming at her was wearing out her limited endurance. She realized that when she reached her limit and failed to block one of Mason's blows it likely *would* injure her. She tried to let one slip in and hit her so he'd stop, but the velocity of Mason's swing frightened her and she danced away, though barely. This caused her panic and she slipped moderately deeply into her dreaded zone. Well then, she decided, she'd just hit him a medium blow to get him to
~~~

acknowledge that she'd actually attacked. She hoped that might get the nightmare over with. As Mason swung a powerful overhead blow she stepped in, deflected it just to her side with the center of her staff and then let the right pad on the end of her staff swing around to lightly strike the side of his head.

~~~

Phil watched in amazement as the large, physically-fit Mason pounded at the slender girl. "Who's it gonna be, you or me? Hit me so's I can feel it!" Mason grunted out that last, and then he slipped and fell down. At least, it looked like he slipped.

Everyone thought, like Phil did, that Mason'd just stumbled somehow. None of them even saw Ell's staff strike him.

Ell dropped to her knees beside Mason. Exhausted, but clinging to her staff to stay upright she said, "Sorry, sorry, *dammit*, I didn't know what else to do!" With big round eyes, she looked over her shoulder at Zymonds and said, "Call the medics! Ma'am? Call the medics!"

Phil stared at Ell, wondering what she was whimpering about. Then a chill rushed over him, leaving his hair standing on end. He slowly realized that Mason wasn't bouncing back to his feet from that little slip. Phil stepped over to look at him and saw blood pouring out of Mason's deformed nose. His headgear was twisted out of kilter and his upper lip was split so wide his upper left canine was visible. Mason's chest still rose and fell, but his lights were well and truly out!

~~~

Cadet Lieutenant Johnson called an ambulance with his AI and had Zymonds take the squad for a couple of laps around the field. Donsaii was crying and didn't look like she could stand up. Johnson let Ell stay behind while they ran. As they ran, Phil watched out of the corner of his eye and saw the MPs asking her and Johnson questions while the ambulance picked up Mason.

The next day the official line was that Mason "deflected one of Donsaii's blows" onto his own head. "Freak accident." Mason was to be chastised for "engaging a cadet in such aggressive combat."

It seemed that no one but Phil really had any idea what'd actually happened.

Phil himself? Cold chills washed over him for days… anytime Donsaii came into view… freezing cold chills. Mason was big, quick, strong, and taught unarmed combat day in and day out, but when he pushed *Donsaii* to her limit she just *took him down*.

Hit him so hard that, even with that heavily padded stick, it was two weeks before he came back on duty.

Maybe what happened to me back in Chapel Hill wasn't so embarrassing after all? Phil did wonder how such a physical combat monster could be such a whuss at running or anything else that required stamina. Was she just putting on?

~~~

They received their milspec AI hardware about then. They'd actually been doing completely without AI for the first few weeks of Basic Training. It seemed pointless to Phil, but he could understand the concept that you could and should learn to function without AI. The milspec hardware was something else though. Back when they'd been fitted for uniforms, molds had been taken of their heads and ear canals. Their new HUDs fit
~~~

their heads like they'd grown there and had two earpieces that fit perfectly into their ear canals, completely occluding them.

They were marched into an auditorium. A slightly chubby officer stepped to the front of the room and said, "Listen up Cadets. You hold in your hands a true high end AI. I'm here to tell you why it's so much better than the civilian pieces of crap you've been wearing. The thin tube on a good civvy earpiece fills about a third of one ear canal and all it does is deliver sound from your AI to you. You may be wearing two earpieces, but really the only reason for having two is so you can get music in stereo.

"*These* custom-fit milspec earpieces completely occlude both ear canals and produce a 30 decibel drop in sound transmission from the outside. They have a mike on the outside that picks up incoming sound and sends it to your AI. The AI takes that incoming sound and compresses it so loud sounds, like explosions and gunshots, are reduced to protect your hearing. Then it plays it back into the depths of your ear canal for you to hear.

"Even better, say you're next to an explosion that has a volume of 160 dB, which could really damage your hearing. That 30 dB drop from the earpiece only gets you down to 130 dB, which is still painfully loud. In that situation, the AI pulls out all the stops and plays an inverse, or out of phase, sound wave into your ear canal to actually cancel even more of that volume. So, on the one hand they're high performance ear protectors. On the other hand, they can, at a simple "enhance hearing" command, increase the volume of quiet sounds. And you can have it enhance certain frequencies to pick up things like breathing, or whispering, or footsteps.

Algorithms for picking up different things are built into the AI, so you'll need training in how to use them.

"Your new AI headbands are custom fit too. A lot of you probably have custom fit headbands, but they're for comfort. These fit so they don't come off if you get knocked around and they're *tough*. You can play rugby in them and, right after a scrum, you'll look up and your HUD screens'll still be right there below your eyebrows."

The instructor demonstrated that the cameras were shock resistant by having them put their headbands on, giving them all a feed off his cameras, then taking his own headband off and whacking it against the lectern. The motion was dizzying, but there wasn't any of the static and fuzz that had perturbed the record of Ell beating the crap out of Phil back in North Carolina.

"Of course, your new cameras see into the infrared and ultraviolet. They can project those images in colors you can see on your HUD. This essentially provides you night vision."

Phil noted that the belt packs containing the CPUs were smaller, heavier, flatter and, the instructor said, more shock resistant than civvy ones too. They came generic so the cadets could download their own AI's personalities and subroutines into them. From there, software mods brought their AI's thought processes up to military standards.

The instructor went on, "You might've noticed that, whenever you change to a new earpiece on your civvy AIs, it messes up your sound perception for a while. That's because your brain learns how the curls and flutes of your external ear shape the sounds you hear and uses that data to determine where sounds are coming from. The sound tube from your AI messes up your perception until you get used to it. Well it's even worse with these milspec earpieces because they alter and process incoming sounds a *lot* more than the simpler effects those little civvy tubes have when they're occluding just a portion of your ear canal. So, for now you're gonna spend all your training time in your new milspec gear. Running in it, fighting in it, sleeping in it. You'll also be having training courses in what the military software we've added to your AI can pull up and display for you."

~~~

Wearing the new headgear day and night quickly got them used to the auditory perception changes and after a few days they once again knew exactly where a sound came from.

Using the infrared vision projected on their HUD at night also took some getting used to. For this, instead of projecting information around the upper periphery of their vision like an AI normally did, the AI actually projected a ghostly version of the world right over the real world they couldn't see in the dark.

~~~

How better to learn to use this stuff than to use it to play sleep-deprived war games at night? The doolies were awakened at midnight and taken off into the forest, with laser sensor webs strapped all over their bodies. M-25s with target-laser under-barrels were in their hands. Ell and Phil's squadron, "G" or "Guts", was up against "F" or "Fox" squadron. Phil was pissed because their squad from Guts got tasked with defending the Guts flag while most of the rest of the squadron was out flitting through the night trying to take the Fox flag. Cadet Captain Andrews had chosen the big-offense, small-defense strategy.

Now, personally Phil favored the offensive himself. He just wanted to be out there offending, rather than stuck back with the single squad that sat on its ass around the flag waiting to be attacked. Their squad's lieutenant was sick so Zymonds was in charge. She'd positioned them loosely in a two-layered circle around the flag bearer. Phil was in the inner layer and the two doolies in front of him were a little guy named Czbarnek and, to his intense irritation, Donsaii. So he's out there as a defender, already pissed. Then he's teamed with someone he doesn't like, who despite Phil's constant rudeness is insufferably nice to him. Finally, they're not even on the front where you'd expect the attack to come from, nope, they're covering the rear quarter. Zymonds' voice came on the push over their AIs, "Any sightings?"

"No" comes back as a routine chorus. But there was a "Yes" mixed in there and so Phil had his AI flash a map in his HUD to see who it was. Donsaii's position was flashing red! "Chuck. Boost infrared." he stared out into the dark over Donsaii's head.

Zymonds came back on, "What're you seein' Donsaii?" She sounded tense. Phil realized that Zymonds was just a year or so older than he was—probably not as blasé as she always acted.

"I'm not sure,"

Phil snorted in disgust to himself, but silently because their mikes were turned up enough to send even sub vocalizations out over their local net.

"Faint movement, I think."

Yeah, sure, what's she thinking with*?* Phil grumbled to himself.

"Yes, couple of movers, tree to tree, heading 67 and 69, about a hundred meters out."

"Chuck. Map." Chuck designated the locations Donsaii'd called out on Phil's HUD map and when he had Chuck flip him back to infrared, he also spotted them as small red marks on his field of view. Donsaii's steady little green mark was just below their position and slightly to the right in his field of view.

Phil didn't see anything out there himself.

Donsaii came back on, "They're flitting again. Permission to take 'em out?"

Zymonds, tersely, "NO! Give me a count."

"Five now."

"Zabrisk, Czbarnek, you see anything?"

Phil almost said no, but then he saw a flicker of motion on his HUD. "Yes Ma'am, faint motion."

"Okay, backup team to left rear quadrant. Donsaii, you take 'em on. The rest of you hold fire until you can pick up targets off their return shots at Donsaii." The words "take 'em" had barely registered on him when Phil's HUD lit up with a rip of five streaks from Ell's laser—he counted them later on an AI replay. Phil thought, *Shit, she's firing on auto; Zymonds'll have her ass.*

Sure enough, the next thing on the net was Zymonds, "Donsaii! Single shots or bursts of three, *you dumb shit*!"

"Yes Ma'am, I am Ma'am."

Phil's thinking to himself, *God damn!* 'Cause he's realizing that she's *just so fast* that she might actually be taking single aimed shots!

~~~

For her part, Ell was in the zone, thinking that in the
~~~

dark, no one'd know what she was doing, or how fast she was moving. It was incredibly fun to just drop deep in the zone and let 'er rip without worrying that someone might get hurt or freak out over her performance.

~~~

Zymonds came back with, "Don't try to bullshit me, Puke. Single shots! And move before someone targets your site." Goosebumps were running up Phil's spine as he realized that none of the attackers had shot back at her. Course it might be because she'd shot at shadows. Or it might be that none of them picked out her location despite the flashes from her M-25. Or... it might be that she hit *all five* with that burst, 'cause a hit turns off your laser and, if you move from where you were when you got hit, the referee AI deducts a bunch of points from your team's score.

"Already moved Ma'am."

Phil didn't see her move, so he thought she was lying. He watched carefully for her to move after her response, wanting to prove her a liar.

~~~

Ell could now see quite a few more intruders. Deep in the zone, she shot the closest, carefully moved to the next, waited, shot, moved to the next, waited and shot that intruder too. That being a burst of three, she held fire and moved over behind the next tree.

~~~

What Phil saw was another burst of three from a spot two meters left of where the first burst came from. This time he did see a flicker of movement as Donsaii moved to the right.
~~~

"SINGLE SHOTS, GODDAMMIT! TAKE THAT GUN OFF AUTO!" Zymonds sounded *really* peeved now.

~~~

Damn it, Ell thought, *she'd said I could use a burst of three.* She said, "Yes Ma'am." *I'll have to slow my firing rate even more, but it's so hard to tell how much time's passing in the zone.*

~~~

Phil stared into the darkness. Another burst of four shots in two pairs came from a new location to the right! Slower yes, but still faster than any normal human being could fire aimed shots. The shots hadn't come from where he thought Ell was, but it couldn't have been anyone else, the other cadets from the squad were all too far from her location.

Before Zymonds could yell at her again, all hell broke loose. It seemed like there was laser fire coming from everywhere. Phil fired a couple of random shots in the direction he'd seen some muzzle flashes and then Chuck said, "You're dead." Sure enough, he looked down at his laser and saw that its ready lights had gone out. Chuck asked, "You want a feed on the battle?"

"Yeah," Phil said, disgustedly. He couldn't go anywhere, so there was nothing to do but watch the battle on the referee AI's map. The map Chuck fed into his HUD put him at the center and their flag back to his right. Sure enough, there were green "F" for Fox designators *everywhere* out there. The major Fox thrust was rolling right over his position!

The hair went up on the back of his neck again. There were also red Fs designating kills *all over* the map in front of Donsaii's position. Chuck was overlaying his real field of view with the HUD map so he saw another flurry of shots from Ell's approximate position and sure enough, four more green Fs switched to red Fs.

About then, someone in Fox ended the battle by capturing the Guts flag. The doolies sat there for a few minutes while Cadet Captain Andrews decided where they'd rally. While he waited, Phil got Chuck to overlay Ell's shots with the red F's out there. As best he could tell—and that's pretty good with a milspec AI working positions out of its memory—by his count all but four of her shots took out targets. The four misses were followed up less than a second later with successful kill shots! Yes, she'd missed, but she *knew* she'd missed and she'd remedied her errors. No one from F troop shot Ell—because she *always* saw and killed them first.

She was still killing F troops right up to the moment the Guts flag went down.

Phil just couldn't absorb what he'd seen—it couldn't be possible, yet he'd been witness to too many of her feats of speed and coordination—they couldn't *all* be flukes.

~~~

As their squad gathered for the march over to where the larger offensive part of the squadron was, Phil steeled himself to hear her bragging about her feat. Sure as hell, he would have been gloating over a performance like that. Instead, she came around, patting the rest of them on the back, saying things like:

"Come on.

"Buck up.

"Next time we'll get 'em.

"They just got lucky."

Phil looked around at the rest of the faces and
~~~

realized that they were all depressed about the loss. Not a single one of them had any idea what Ell'd done and, believe it or not, she wasn't pointing it out to them!

Zymonds came up behind her, livid. "Donsaii! Yeah, you *better* try to cheer up this squad. Maybe they'll forget who started blasting off like a movie star with endlessammo. Jaysus! How many shots you got left in that M-25 anyway?"

"Ma'am," she looked down at her laser. She looked back up at her, "Five shots Ma'am."

"So you only fired off thirty-five shots? Jeez. I thought it'd be worse than that, the way you were blasting away."

"No Ma'am." Phil waited for her to point out that she'd killed thirty-one Fox troops with those thirty-five shots but, no, she just stood there at attention. Phil thought she'd at least point out that none of the Fox squadron doolies got past her position. But she didn't. Even though a grudging admiration for Donsaii had been blossoming inside Phil, he wasn't about to point Ell's astonishing feat out to Zymonds himself.

Phil realized that, although Zymonds was *acting* pissed, she wasn't really. None of the upperclassmen rode Donsaii as hard as they rode the rest of the doolies. Phil just didn't understand it. He himself didn't actually *hate* her anymore, but he certainly couldn't see what everyone else was so damned moony about.

"Form up!" The squad ran to their places and Phil consoled himself that he didn't actually have time to point out Ell's incredible feat for her, though truth to tell he'd had plenty of time before Zymonds formed them up for the march. As they marched, he thought about how someone was bound to figure it out. After all, a review of the battle would show all those Fox "dead" in front of her position. It looked to him like the main Fox push was right over Donsaii, and the ones who actually got through to take the Guts flag were a few stragglers to the right side of that thrust.

Then Phil thought there must be some kind of targeting efficiency rating that the computers calculated for the staff. That would surely thrust her feat into the limelight. Later he realized that the system probably hadn't been set up to recognize whose laser killed which opponent, so they wouldn't be able to do such an analysis. Not expecting any marksmanship feats, they wouldn't have the AIs set to notice the kind of event that had just happened.

In any case, Phil kept quiet and no one else seemed to be aware of the astonishing shooting feat that'd just happened in their midst.

Actually, the cadets in Guts squadron were mostly just bummed out by losing.

~~~

Phil did have Chuck check to see how Donsaii had done in their live firing practice with a real M-25. That was the weapon that the laser shooting imitations were supposed to match in weight and feel. Actual M-25s had been lightened and the laser hung coaxially under the barrel to create the practice weapons. The lasers even fired blanks to give a kick and a flash of light like a real M-25. Donsaii's numbers on the firing range were very good, but she wasn't the best in their little squad.

The whole thing *just* didn't make sense to Phil.

***
~~~

Donsaii might be kicking ass in combat situations but her performance on endurance tasks continued to be laughably poor. They went for a long run one morning each week and she was guaranteed to be full of fire at the beginning, dying in the middle and dropping out, puking and practically being carried before it was done.

On Friday they were up in the dark before dawn, then fell out onto the training field. Anderson stepped up to the front of the formation and bellowed, "You Pukes ready to run?"

"Yes sir!" the squad bellowed back, Donsaii's voice louder than anyone else's.

"Donsaii?"

"Yes sir!"

"You really think you're ready for a ten mile run?" You could hear the grin in his voice.

Even Phil, who by now was in great condition, groaned inside at the thought of a ten mile run.

To his amazement he heard Donsaii cheerfully reply, "Yes sir!"

Anderson grinned at her and said, "No shit Cay-det?" Phil was astounded, upperclassmen never smiled at doolies.

"No sir!"

"Now you *know* you're gonna be dyin' before we go three miles and dead before we go eight?"

"Not this time sir!"

Anderson threw his head back and laughed. "Gotta admire the attitude! Who's gonna pick her dyin' ass up and drag her along for the last half of this run?"

"We will sir!" the entire squad bellowed in unison. Ell grinned sheepishly. Phil was startled to realize that they all cheerfully meant it too. Somehow, while he hadn't been paying attention, her constantly positive attitude had resulted in her becoming an object of affection for the other cadets!

All except one.

Sure as Hell, she cheerfully led the singing for the first half mile, then gasped out the chant for the next couple of miles, then different cadets started pulling up beside her to let her hold onto their shoulders. By the end of the run she was practically being carried, her arms over shoulders on either side of her. There were so many volunteers that Phil never got put on the spot to have to help her himself, though he did help a couple of the other weak links.

An hour after the run she was actively making fun of herself for being such a wuss, and carefully thanking everyone who'd helped her on the run.

Zymonds came around to give her hell, "Donsaii!"

"Yes Ma'am?"

"You've got to be the worst runner I've ever seen!"

"No doubt, Ma'am!" she said cheerfully.

Despite herself Zymonds started grinning. "Are you ever gonna do any better?"

"Absolutely, Ma'am!" she grinned back.

"But, you're always gonna be terrible aren't you?"

"No doubt, Ma'am!"

Zymonds toned her voice down. "I'm worried about you Cadet. You might not make it for the six minute mile at the end of Basic, you know that?"

Ell's shoulders drooped. "Yes Ma'am. I'll just have to do the best I can and hope I make it."

Zymonds shook her head and wandered off to organize their marching drill. Phil shook his head. Anyone else but Donsaii, and Zymonds would have been ripping their head off and crapping down their neck.

But it's Donsaii, so the cadet sergeant says she's worried about her?!

~~~

On the next to the last day of Basic, Squadron Captain Andrews marched them out to the testing field where everyone passed their minimums of pushups, pull-ups, sit-ups and other fitness requirements. When it came time for them to do the mile run, Ell lined up at the back of the squad so she wouldn't slow anyone else down. Cadet Lieutenant Johnson held up the start of the run and bellowed. "Donsaii!"

"Yes sir?" she answered from her spot at the back.

"Get up here. We have a spot reserved for you at the front inner corner of the track." When Ell got there he leaned close and said quietly, "Zymonds has this theory that you need to start fast like you do on the obstacle course. That way you'll have a lead that'll let you drag the last lap or so and still make it under six minutes. What do you think of that?"

The upperclassman's concern touched her. Her voice husky, Ell said, "That might help sir."

"Ok, you go for it then. We didn't want your classmates blocking you from doing it. If it doesn't work, I'll make sure you get another chance to run it at a steady pace tomorrow."

After a summer of endurance activities Ell had learned that she was good for about three minutes of high performance activity, but beyond that she'd lose steam and by ten minutes she'd be having marked difficulty. If the requirement had been for two, or five or ten miles she probably couldn't have made it. Importantly, she'd also learned that it only took
~~~

minutes to recover, even after long runs. Surprisingly, when she went deep into the zone and stayed there for very long, it left her tired for longer than a distance run did.

So, she carefully repressed her zone. When the starting buzzer sounded she took off at a fast pace for her non-zone state, though nothing like she could've run if she were *in* the zone. After a lap she saw she was far out in front and worried that this was a bad strategy. Nonetheless, she resolved to keep to it since they'd promised her another try tomorrow if it didn't work. By the end of the third 400 meter lap she'd actually lapped many of the slower runners, but fatigue began to slow her down. Part way through the last lap her stamina was gone and the slower runners were "un-lapping" her. When she finished the fourth lap—plus a little—to reach the mile finish line most of the squad had passed her slow slog, but she was still well under six minutes. The members of the squadron that'd already finished were gathered to clap her across and help her walk it out.

Cadet Lieutenant Johnson stopped by and said, "You should try out for the track team! You did that first 800 meters under two minutes. A time like that would definitely get you on the team."

Ell, gave it little thought. Her plan was to focus on academics.

Chapter Three

Basic Training hadn't really gone on forever.

It'd just *seemed* that way.

Eventually they graduated with a small ceremony and the regular academic school year began. The rest of the upper-class cadets came back and the doolies were formed into their real squadrons. It turned out that Zabrisk and Donsaii's squad from the Guts training squadron were all going into 22nd squadron.

As expected, their new 22nd squadron upperclassmen greeted the doolies as if they couldn't believe they'd been saddled with such losers.

They settled into a school year made up of early formations, training runs, breakfast, classes from eight till noon, lunch, and two more hours of study halls and special training, then physical training or intramural sports, then dinner, and then study till lights out. Somehow, in the nonexistent time left over, they were supposed to keep their shoes polished, their rooms spic and span and show motivation by performing various feats to indicate their *esprit de corps*.

The upperclassmen dutifully made the lives of the mere doolies miserable, holding surprise inspections, taking them out for midnight runs and constantly yelling at them in formation. Meals were a hell where they ate at attention, recited inane details from the careers of previous members of the 22nd squadron and were generally harassed whenever possible.

"You squats, pull your plugs!" It was their Table Commander, Cadet Captain Alston. Alston was at the head of the table and Phil was at the foot with two other doolies on either side of him. They dutifully pulled out earpieces so they wouldn't be able to get any answers from their AIs. "Okay. Zabrisk. What rank did former 22nd Squadron Cadet Seddon achieve?"

Seddon was a Medal of Honor winner who'd come out of 22nd Squadron, that much Phil knew. Seddon'd died winning his medal though, going down with his stricken plane, but keeping it stable enough that everyone else was able to bail out. Phil knew what plane he'd been flying, which engines were out, that there had been extensive damage to the tail control surfaces, and who his copilot had been. But what rank? No clue. So, he took a WAG (Wild Ass Guess) based on the fact that most pilots were fairly young and thus held relatively junior rank, "Captain, sir!"

"Very good Zabrisk. If your two classmates are that knowledgeable, you might get out of this evening's bombing mission." He smirked, "I see we're having fudge sundaes."

Shit! Phil's heart sank. "Bombing missions" involved having one of the doolies at the table serve as a target, head leaned back and mouth open. Another Dooley served as the bomber. Blindfolded with a napkin and holding a large spoonful of ice cream, the bomber moved the ice cream around in the air over the target's face. The third Dooley served as the bombardier, calling out directions to the bomber as to where to move the spoon and when to dump the ice cream, hopefully into the target's mouth. It was a lucky target who got any of the ice cream in his mouth; generally it went all over his or her face. The target usually was the one sitting at the foot, Phil's current position. He had on his last clean shirt! "Smith!"

"Yes sir!"

"Who was Seddon's co-pilot?"

Mary J Mabry! Phil thought emphatically at Smith.

Smith sweated a few seconds, then said, "Sir, I do not know, sir!"

"One 'sir' to a sentence squat! Is that *too* difficult?"

"No sir!"

"Well, boys, it looks like they need to make a bombing run, eh? Zabrisk!"

"Yes sir!"

"You're sittin' in the target chair."

"Yes sir!"

"Now it don't seem fair, you bein' the target, when it was Smith that couldn't answer the question, does it?"

Phil knew he'd be damned if he blamed his classmate, but the question had sounded rhetorical, "No sir!"

"So. Are you thinking Smith should be the target?" There was a dangerous tone in the table captain's voice.

"No sir!" *Definitely the correct answer*, he thought to himself.

"So, you volunteerin' to be the target?"

"Yes sir!" *Hell no*, he thought to himself, but he didn't even *think* it very loud.

Minutes later, Phil's head was tipped back, a napkin inadequately covering his shirt. Smith began dumping loads of ice cream and chocolate syrup all over him to directional shouts from Dilinski.

Not a drop went in his mouth, but his only clean shirt was ruined.

The upperclassmen were thoroughly entertained.

There were bombing missions at a lot of tables that night and later he heard a guy from Donsaii's table talking. She'd been assigned as bombardier. The guy telling the story had been the target and he spoke in awe of how only the first spoonful of ice cream partially missed his mouth. She'd carefully directed the bomber's course and speed, then had him drop on the count of three. "I think the only reason the first one missed is 'cause it came off the spoon slower than she expected. Course, I'm still a mess from the splashes." The listening group was divided among those who thought she'd been *very* lucky and those who were trying to understand and comprehend her strategy in directing her bomber and dropping on a count.

Phil? He tried to ignore the hair prickling down the back of his neck. Again!

~~~

Ell'd never needed a lot of sleep. Three or four hours had always been it, then she'd be awake again. She'd always gone to bed at midnight to keep from freaking out her mother, but she'd taken a lot of her advanced math classes on the net in the early morning hours from three to six when she couldn't get back to sleep. She'd learned not to talk about it with kids her age. They typically slept a lot more than that and tended to decide she was weird. When she slept over with friends she'd lay awake in the dark, working her current math problems in her head. Usually her attempts to create a dimensional math that could correlate quantum entanglement and the double-slit experiment to reality. Reality, plus that one extra dimension through which Ell hypothesized that the particles were actually connected. The summer exertions of basic training had
~~~

had her sleeping four to five hours except when they got her up for night training. Now that the school year had started, she had less physical exertion to exhaust her, so she was back to sleeping three hours a night. This gave her time to work on keeping her room and clothes really sharp before lights out. After lights out she put her pillow next to her head so the light from her HUD wouldn't bother Joy Denson, who'd become her roommate. Using this strategy she could study for her classes *after* lights out.

She still had time she could spend on her odd theories because keeping up with her studies didn't take too long at the rate Ell could read. Until then she'd been trying to picture a photon going through the double slit experiment. When she'd pictured it in the past she'd viewed it as if it were two photons, or half photons going through the two slits, but connected beneath the plane of the experiment by a kind of U-shaped connector through her additional dimension. Now she realized that she could picture the single photon in the slit experiment as spread out like thousands of photons all connected through her tiny dimension, allowing the thousands to act like a wave that then coalesced on a single location when they arrived at the receiver. This had her so excited that she succeeded in ignoring her alarm until Joy shook her shoulder and said, "Get up sleepyhead!" While Ell brushed her teeth Joy said, "We need to do some kind of spirit thing for 22nd Squadron."

Ell spit in the sink, "We?"

"Yeah, but something better than arranging sheets on the side of the mountain to spell '22,' that's lame."

"Okay, what's your idea?"

"I don't have one. I just know we need one that's *not*

lame."

~~~

Phil woke to an insistent quiet knocking at his door. It was freaking 2AM! When he opened his door, Ell stood there with her trademarked crooked grin. Jason and Joy stood behind her, looking about as exhausted as Phil felt. "We've had a great idea!" she started brightly.

"There *are* no good ideas at this time of night." Phil grumbled.

"I ordered this paint…"

~~~

Soon Phil and Jason were holding Ell up at arm's length against the west wall of the parade ground while she sprayed paint she swore was water soluble onto the granite facing. Joy stood lookout. Then it was Jason, standing on Phil's shoulders as Ell scrambled up over both of their bodies and stood on Jason's shoulders to lay some kind of sensor device on top of the wall.

~~~

In the morning, despite still feeling irked at getting up in the middle of the night, Phil looked eagerly at the west wall. There was nothing there! Had it rained and washed it away? He looked at Ell. She winked at him!

They were called to attention and his eyes were turned away, but the sun was rising. As more light slanted across the grounds he began to hear some murmurs among the upperclassmen, then some chuckles amongst his own squadron. They were about to march to breakfast when the ripping sound of the string of firecrackers set off by Ell's photosensor directed everyone's attention to the west wall. There,
~~~

neat letters spelling out "22nd Raptors" were now visible wherever sunlight had struck the wall. A lusty cheer went up from 22nd squadron.

Their cadet captain called them back to attention. With a tremendous frown he said, "I don't suppose I'll *ever* find out who was responsible for that defacement of Academy property so I'm going to be giving 10 demerits to every one of the doolies in this squadron!" There was a long pause, then he broke into a big grin, "And I'm deducting 15 demerits from each of the 22nd Raptor doolies for a Kick Ass performance this morning!" A spontaneous cheer went up and they marched in to breakfast in high spirits. Sure enough, as they left breakfast they saw the groundskeepers successfully washing the light activated paint off the wall with a hose.

~~~

Phil may have had his problems with Donsaii, but he seemed to be just about the only one who didn't adore her. The upperclassmen hardly ever jumped her shit. Even Phil had to admit that she never seemed to have a hair out of place at inspections or, for that matter at any other time. Her uniforms fit as if they'd been custom tailored for her, making her look *so* good people quietly said she should be on the Academy recruitment website. It was rumored she actually tailored her uniforms herself. At night, with a flashlight, under a blanket after lights out.

Her roommate, Joy Denson, confided to Jason that Ell did practically *all* the work involved in keeping their room spotless for inspections. Denson was having trouble keeping up with her class work. Ell'd volunteered to do their military spit and polish so Joy
~~~

could have time to study! Joy said Ell was up all hours of the night doing extra projects, hardly seemed to sleep, rarely studied and, damn it, was always in a good mood! Joy worried Ell couldn't be passing her classes with as little time as she spent on them, but Ell had repeatedly reassured Joy she was doing okay.

Despite his mixed feelings about Ell, Phil thought she looked even better than when he'd first met her. All the physical conditioning made her even leaner and more fit appearing. Phil liked big breasts, but admitted that they'd have seemed out of place on Donsaii's slender frame. He couldn't help admiring her willowy yet muscular legs when they went out for training runs. Short military hair agreed with her, outlining her delicate features and somehow making those brilliant green eyes stand out even more brightly against her strawberry blond complexion. Her constant smile and apparently permanent good mood meant that people just plain liked being around her.

Phil couldn't believe Ell could be so consistently cheerful considering the long hours she was supposed to be putting in. The only time she didn't smile was when she was being dressed down by an upperclassman. After all, a smile during a scolding pissed them off. However, since she rarely got in trouble by herself, the dressing downs she received were almost always as part of a group of other doolies.

It wasn't all peaches and cream. Some of the other women cadets were jealous, even though many of them also had tales to tell about how Donsaii had helped them with this or that problem. Because of this, there were a lot of mixed messages in the rumor mill about Ell, but they didn't seem to consolidate one way or the other.

Even though Phil's feelings about her weren't all warm and fuzzy, it irritated him immensely when he stood behind a couple of the upperclassmen from 16th squadron at an intramural soccer game. One of them leaned to the other, "Hey, how about that hot doolie they've got in 22nd squadron?"

There being no doubt in his mind who they were talking about, Phil wasn't surprised to hear, "Oh yeaahh! The cute chick with the strawberry hair? I'd like to give her some remedial training myself!"

Phil wondered if there was anything he could do to put the upperclassmen in their places. There turned out to be no need to intervene though, because the conversation took its own strange course.

"Better be careful asswipe, she's the doolie who took out Sergeant Mason with a pugil stick this summer!"

The guy snorted. "I heard about that. That was some kind of volleyball girl, right? They're big."

"Nope, it was Donsaii."

"Even if it was, it was some kind of freak accident, right?"

"Ok... You bet. Sure. Let me know when *you're* ready to 'freak accident' the Sarge into the hospital. I'll be happy to set you up a match."

~~~

The 1st year cadets finally got a weekend pass to go into town for a little R&R. Some of the doolies in their squadron had family that came into town for a visit. The lucky ones had a girlfriend or boyfriend show up. Most of them though, had no one but each other. Jason and Phil planned to head into Colorado Springs together and see what kind of nightlife they could scare up. It'd been
~~~

four months since he'd chased any skirt, what with the strict no fraternization rules currently in effect at the Academy. They weren't even supposed to think of the women cadets as female, though they could hardly avoid it.

However, if they got caught fooling around with another cadet, it was their ass, so Phil had pretty much stayed away. Anyway, the only one in 22nd squadron that really caught his eye was Donsaii, and he knew all too well what'd happen if he put the moves on her.

So, all things considered, Phil was really looking forward to a weekend out.

Jason showed up at his door at the appointed time, carrying a bag with his civvies. Damned if he didn't have Denson with him! Jason and Joy stepped across the threshold into his room and broke out of their positions of attention. *Sheeit*, Phil thought, *I'm gonna be the third wheel on a date!* "Hey, you two goin' sweet on me?" he asked.

Denson looked at the floor and Jason scuffed a toe and said, "Naw, man, Denson here, she and I were just talkin' about weekend plans and thought maybe we could share the cost of taxis around town to a few places."

Yeah sure, Phil thought, but decided he'd play along before Jason died of embarrassment. "Okay, let's go then."

"Wait one, Donsaii'll be here in a sec."

Phil hardly had time for his heart to sink before another knock came on the door. Phil opened the door and Ell stood there at attention. Disgustedly, he waved her in. She stepped in, broke attention, grinned crookedly at him and said, "Back in Chapel Hill I *told* you we'd go out again at an academy."

His mind whirled; he vaguely remembered something like that, Right before she busted his face! *Has she forgiven me? Am I supposed to have forgiven her? Do I forgive her?*

Phil didn't know how or, later, even *if* he responded, but they headed into town. They weren't allowed cars, but a regular bus ran into town on the weekend to keep them from hitchhiking. They changed into civvies in a bathroom, had pizza at a local joint, and played some games at an arcade. Phil carefully watched Ell play and she performed no superhuman feats. She played very well, he'd grant you, but none of the unearthly performances he'd witnessed in the past. He won the game of air hockey she challenged him to. They wandered around the campus of Colorado College. Jason talked about trying to get some beer, but they were all under age and fake ID apps wouldn't install on their new military AIs. Secretly Phil felt relieved not to do something that was illegal and could get him a bunch of demerits. He knew he'd certainly have succumbed to peer pressure and put away some beer with the rest of them if Jason'd been able to get in any.

Jason didn't push the idea very hard, so they went to a nonalcoholic club that catered to underage college kids. They all agreed it was lame, but they hung out there for a while anyway. Jason went out to dance with Denson, leaving Phil alone in the booth with Donsaii. The more he thought about it the more pissed off he got. He really wanted to chase the ladies in this place, but here he was, stuck with Donsaii, the one chick in the entire world that he couldn't make time with! Ell sat there and stared at him while he stared out around the club, essentially looking at everything *except* Ell.

Eventually Donsaii leaned over to him and shouted

over the beat, "Wanna dance?"

"Nah. This place is *too* lame." *Actually,* he thought, *I could have a great time here if you weren't with me.*

"Hey, you *still* pissed about Chapel Hill?"

"Nah. Gotta find the can." He got up and beat a retreat toward the restrooms. After he hit the head he cruised back around the bar the long way, checking out the talent.

A real cutie caught his eye. She had brunette hair and it spilled down to the small of her back, a sure sign she wasn't a cadet. At that moment proof that she wasn't a cadet made her much more attractive , so he ambled her direction. She looked up and caught his eye on her, "Hi." *No genius to that line,* he thought, mentally kicking himself.

"Hi yourself. You a Zoomie?" she grinned.

Some people used the term "Zoomie" derogatorily when speaking of the cadets, but he didn't think she meant it that way. "Yeah," he shrugged, "newly minted."

"Oooohh, how cute." She winked at him, "A doolie?"

That didn't sound as good. He realized that she was older, maybe twenty to his nineteen, a chasm at that age, especially when the woman's older than you. "Yeah," he said, turning to survey the bar in preparation to beating a retreat.

"Carmine!" she oozed, "Look what just tried to pick me up." Brightly, "It's a Doooolie."

Phil turned back. "Carmine" was a behemoth. At least six foot six, he probably had a "Wide Load" sign on his back with you appropriate flashers on his shoulders. His brows crinkled together, actually, his eyebrows weren't separate, just a single brow, but it *had* developed deep vertical furrows in the middle. His narrow set eyes were focused on Phil and emitting a couple thousand watts. Phil, waved his hands, palms out, "Hey, I didn't mean nothin'. Just saying hello." Phil was thinking to himself that as a championship wrestler, he should have nothing to fear, but this guy was B-I-G and looked like he was in shape too.

"You thinkin' you can make time with my girl, puke?"

The brunette lit up, she obviously loved this stuff.

Puke! Phil thought. He was sick of being called a puke by the upperclassmen. He couldn't talk back to them, but he could sure as hell talk back to *this* asshole. Phil took a deep breath to do so, but suddenly his arms were full of Donsaii. She'd actually leaped up onto him and thrown her arms around his neck and her legs around his waist.

"Phil!" Ell said brightly, "I'm so glad I found you again, I'm ready for that dance now!" She leaned in close to whisper in his ear, "And if you get in a fight with that man-mountain, it'll bust up this place and the police'll be all up *in* your ass. Enough demerits'll stack up for you to march tours till next summer." She dropped off him and stepped off toward the dance floor, dragging him by the wrist. He allowed himself to be led away without looking back.

It was a slow dance and Ell put her arms loosely up around his neck saying, "Sorry, I haven't danced much, so I really don't know how."

Phil clumsily put his hands on her hips. In truth, as he looked back on it later, a little fearful of how she might react. They swayed to the music. He noticed her hips felt very firm… and *very* nice.

Ell said, "I saw what that little bitch did. I know you could've taken that big guy, being a wrestler and all, but it would've brought a lot of trouble and I thought maybe I could defuse the situation."

"Yeah... yeah, you're right. Thanks." was all Phil could think to say. He wished he didn't sound so surly.

He daydreamed about that dance when awake and had real dreams about it when he was asleep for weeks after that. But he couldn't bring himself to ask her to dance again.

She didn't ask him again either.

He knew he was a fool.

As are all men sometimes.

~~~

After that one dance Phil and Ell returned to sit in the booth a while longer, watching Jason dancing with Joy. They didn't say word one to one another. Ell felt crushed. She'd *known* Phil would hate being rescued from that situation, *especially* by her. But, though she'd considered it, she'd found she just couldn't let him get in a lot of trouble when she might be able to prevent the fight in the first place.

~~~

For his part Phil felt like he couldn't leave Donsaii again after she'd saved his ass with the man-mountain, but he resented her for having ruined his shot at picking up some other girl. As he thought back on it later, his sitting there pretty much ruined her chances of meeting someone who wasn't scared shitless of her like he was. They were both relieved when Joy and Jason came over and suggested they "blow this dump."

Phil thought they were going back out to the Academy, but Jason wanted to stay out in the free world for the rest of the weekend. Turned out that this meant, "We should all crash in some cheap motel for the night, then wander around Colorado Springs some more tomorrow."

Yeah, Phil thought to himself, *you think you can score some sack time with Denson, you sumbitch.* But he didn't want to be the weak weenie that ran back to base either. Then Ell said, "I don't know..."

Of course, the small town puritan doesn't want to be stuck in a motel room with a horny bastard like me, Phil thought. So, even though he really wanted to go back to base, he said, "Sure, I'll cough up a share. I can crash on the floor."

Ell didn't want to go back to base by herself and they were too cheap to get two rooms. So Phil wound up lying on the floor on one side of the bed, with Jason on the floor on the other side while Ell and Joy took the bed. Joy slipped off the bed on Jason's side and she and Jason quietly hooked up. Not quietly enough. Phil thought he was horny before, but it didn't compare to the way he felt after lying there all night listening to J&J quietly grunting and moaning.

He couldn't help thinking about the marvelous, but untouchable girl still lying up on the bed.

There was no way Phil would ever go after *her* again though.

At one point during that interminable night, he realized that it was fall and must be close to the one-year anniversary of the incident when they first met.

~~~

Phil didn't get much sleep and felt like crap the next morning. Joy and Jason looked a mite peaked too, but not Donsaii. Oh no, she was bright and perky, full of energy and wanting to eat breakfast at the ungodly
~~~

hour of 0900. *First time in five months we've had a chance to sleep in and* she's *up at the crack of dawn!* They finally had breakfast at a Waffle House about 10 in the morning. Then Jason suggested Ell and Phil could check out the park next door while he and Joy went back to the room to "pack."

Ell would have none of it, saying she'd help them pack up.

Phil practically had to drag her out to the park with him.

~~~

Phil and Ell sat in awkward silence on a park bench for a while, but then finally had kind of a nice talk. Later he couldn't really remember what they talked about, but he did recall it was pleasant and warm and how he'd thought she wasn't such a bitch after all.

~~~

Jason and Joy took an hour and a half to pack the few things they had in the room but still managed to forget Jason's toothbrush by the sink. The four of them spent that pleasant fall day wandering around Colorado Springs, but all too soon they headed back out to the Academy to start the grind all over again.

***

Jamal saw the light glowing in the front room of his apartment as he walked up. His stomach began to knot. He wasn't sure how anyone had gotten in, but had no doubt that it was the work of his masters. Their contacts with him had never been the cause of much joy. He coded the lock and stepped inside, not at all surprised to see a stranger sitting in the dimness in one corner of the room. "Hello."

"Are you comfortable here in the big American university?" The man spoke Arabic.

Jamal responded in kind. "Comfortable enough. Do you have a message for me?"

"Kill an American."

"What!?" Jamal's voice broke a little.

"You heard the first time. Do you question your orders now?"

"What? No! But who? And why? To what purpose?"

"Some believe that you are becoming too comfortable here." The man stood and walked to where Jamal stood. "They believe that perhaps the great Satan himself is seducing you. Could that be?"

"No!"

The man drove his fist into Jamal's stomach, doubling him over, then allowing him to drop to the floor. Unable to breath, Jamal gasped for breath.

The man said, "Then do *not* question your orders! I will be back in a week. You will show me proof that you've killed an American."

The man let himself out as Jamal got his first few small gasps of air.

***

Phil was in Advanced Math 202, having tested out of the standard doolie courses 101 and 102 and 2nd year class 201. At first he was quite proud of being one of the only two doolies he knew who'd jumped over three semesters to Math 202. His family, himself included, had always been good at math and his weakness on the admission tests had been in soft subjects like English and Literature. But 202 was hard! He'd never had a math course he thought was difficult before and his score on a recent quiz felt like a hard slap in the face. Now he'd been called in to see the instructor!

"Cadet Zabrisk reporting as ordered sir."

"Sit down Zabrisk." His professor waved vaguely at the chairs in his small office.

Phil wasn't sure if he was actually allowed to sit in the presence of a real captain. After a hesitant movement toward the chair, he remained standing.

"Go ahead, sit!" the captain said, "I forget how timid you freshmen are; don't get many of you in my classes."

Phil sat, but compromised by sitting at attention like he did in the dining hall.

"You're having trouble in the class? A lot of doolies do when they test into it."

"Yes sir, but I'll catch up."

"No doubt, but I don't want you getting buried. It'd be a shame to have to ship you back to 201. How about a little help?"

"Help sir?"

"Sure, a few sessions with a tutor might dig you out of your hole before it gets too deep."

"Tutor, sir?"

"You haven't heard about the tutoring program?"

"No sir."

"It's another way you can work off demerits. You help cadets in a subject you're good at instead of marching tours. You yourself could tutor in 101 or 102 once you get out of trouble in 202. If you like, I can set you up with a tutor. Usually it's an upperclassman in a neighboring squadron. They don't want you to be tutored by someone who's also responsible for your discipline. If you had a classmate in your own squadron who was advanced enough, they'd tutor you so it could be someone you knew, but there wouldn't *be* a doolie advanced enough to tutor 202."

"Thank you sir."

"Good, I'll put you in for it and the computer will assign a one-on-one tutor for you. You'll get a message through your AI to report to a room in study hall for it. Dismissed."

~~~

Phil went to his afternoon intramural session with mixed feelings. He feared any time he spent with a tutor might be wasted time. Time that would have been better spent studying on his own. Especially with a tutor who was pissed to be working off demerits. And of course, in upperclassman would probably treat him like crap anyway.

During dinner Chuck whispered in his ear, "Report to study hall, room 543 at 1930 hours for your tutoring session." *Damn, they were prompt!*

~~~

When Phil appeared in room 543 at the appointed time he was stunned to see Donsaii sitting there at the table. He had no idea that she was in Math 202! "What are *you* doing here, I thought these things were one-on-one?"

Ell looked embarrassed. "Are you here for a Math 202 tutorial session?"

"Yeah," he said disgustedly, dropping into a chair across from her at the little table. "Shoulda' known 'one-on-one' was too good to be true." He felt he'd adequately hidden his dismay that she was also in 202.

He'd always thought that, despite her phenomenal athletic feats, at least he was *way* smarter than she was. For sure smarter in math than anyone from Donsaii's hick town. Actually it seemed pretty surprising that her small town high school would have had the Advanced Placement math curriculum to let her place out of 101 or 102, much less 201!

~~~

Ell felt horrified! Despite their terrible start, she really liked Phil. Sometimes she wondered why and hoped it wasn't just because he looked so good without his shirt. She didn't want to be so shallow as to fall for him on physical attraction alone. His interactions with the other cadets were humorous and good spirited and everyone thought he was a lot of fun. It troubled her no end that he was so standoffish with her. This tutoring thing worried her because she knew he was proud. He'd surely be sensitive about being shown up. She hadn't had any idea he was in 202. If she had, she'd never have listed herself as available to tutor that level!

~~~

Ell hadn't said anything so Phil looked over at her. She looked a little pinched and out of sorts. "This may be a mistake..."

"Oh, you aren't in 202?" He kind of hoped his relief didn't show in his voice.

"Uh, no... I'm working off demerits for painting the West Wall." Ell practically whispered, as if saying it quietly would make it less offensive.

"*You're* my tutor for 202!?" Phil was aghast.

"Yeah, sorry." She grimaced, "We can get you assigned to someone else."

Phil's stomach knotted up. How in the Hell had she gotten so far ahead?! "How?" He asked, "Morehead City schools couldn't have the kind of AP classes that'd get you past any of the math here at the Academy could they?"

Ell made an embarrassed little shrug, then blurted, "No. I'm just kind of a math freak." She burbled on, "I like it so much I study this stuff on my own. It's easy for me 'cause I'm so weird I enjoy it. Then testing placed me out." She stood and picked up her slate. "Sorry. You shouldn't have to be tutored by one of your own classmates."

Phil felt a little tingle over his scalp. *Just kind of a math freak, huh? That's not the only freaky thing about her...* He rubbed his head sheepishly. "Naw, that's okay. I just hope you can help me get my head around this crap. What's the deal on the demerits, I thought we didn't get any?"

"The commandant came down on the Squadron. He told Captain Ayers that somebody 'needed to march some tours for that stunt.' I heard about it so I volunteered. After all, painting the wall was my idea. Besides, I don't mind tutoring. I always understand things better after I explain them to someone else."

Phil felt a little guilty. "You shouldn't have gotten stuck with it alone. I can take some demerits too."

"Aw, that's a nice offer. But really, someone had to do it and it doesn't bother me. If you don't mind having me as a tutor, what are you having problems with in 202?"

Phil laid out his e-slate, "Here's what I'm having trouble with." By the end of the hour he was bemused to realize that she'd explained the vector translation equations and the following math so succinctly and so clearly that he actually wondered why he'd been having trouble with it to begin with.

~~~

By the end of the week Phil had asked enough discrete questions that he'd determined Donsaii wasn't in *any* freshman level classes. Jason had asked Joy and Joy had talked to Ell. She'd found out that Ell was not only taking quite a few 2nd year classes but more than half of her load was 3rd year classes! And, she was killing them with a 4.0 GPA! When Joy'd asked about it Ell had, believe it or not, asked Joy to keep it quiet, "Because she didn't want the other cadets thinking she was weird."

***

Jamal dithered for a few days. Despite years of swearing he stood ready to kill Americans by the thousand—and somehow even feeling as if he already had—he found that the thought of actually *murdering* another human being in cold blood, one who'd done him no harm, offended his soul. *What soul?* He asked himself over and over. *I'm supposed to be a soulless killer!*

He considered fleeing into the vast anonymity of America. Only briefly. As he reminded himself, he really did want to avenge Aki and his own family. As he lay sweating in his bed he called up memories of Aki twitching in the dirt. Memories of the beetle headed soldier attempting to rape his mother. Memories of finally pushing back the box he cowered under and going out to view the ruined carcasses of his mother
~~~

and grandfather. His resolve strengthened and he put out of his mind the many kindnesses done for him by his new friends in this country. Yet, he could not bring himself to contemplate killing someone he knew. Or anyone he had to look in the eye.

Four of the five days grace had passed before Jamal developed a workable plan. Using cash he purchased work gloves at a hardware store on Grant Avenue. Later that afternoon he put on dark clothing and walked down Speedway to where it crossed over I-10. He stood on the overpass, watching the flow of traffic and dropping pebbles onto the cars as they went past. After some experimentation, he chose an exact spot on the freeway below. If a car was at that spot when he dropped the pebble, the falling pebble struck its windshield as it went under the bridge.

He walked back down off the overpass, put on his gloves and stole a concrete block from a construction site a hundred meters away. One of the hollow ones, the hole making a good handle as he trudged back up to the overpass. Dark had fallen. He looked down at the flow of car lights passing beneath him and centered himself over the left side of an oncoming lane. He heaved the block up onto the rail, waited till a set of lights passed his mark and pushed the block off.

The block disappeared in the dim light. For a moment he thought he'd miscalculated—but the physics of gravity remained predictable as ever. The driver's side of the windshield exploded in a spray of glass. When the lights of the vehicle came out from under the other side of the bridge they'd swerved into the next lane. In a moment the vehicle rolled over and began to tumble down the freeway as headlights swerved every which way to avoid it. He wondered if the car had been under manual control rather than AI. Or perhaps, an injury had caused the driver to twist the wheel. Even so, he was surprised the AI hadn't been able to take over and prevent the driver's swerve from crossing lanes and rolling the vehicle. Alarms were screaming, but by then Jamal had walked most of the way down off the overpass and could no longer see what was happening. He threw the gloves into the trash bin at a Circle K nearly a mile from where he'd obtained the block.

He walked miserably back to his apartment.

He passed a strip joint on the way and briefly considered going inside—after all, hadn't his soul already been corrupted as much as it could possibly be?

Chapter Four

The sportscasters would later say that Ell started serious gymnastics during her first year at the Academy. This made it sound like she'd been a non-serious amateur before that year. Well she *had* in fact done gymnastics before… for two years between the ages of three and five. Then her dad died and her mom could no longer afford to send her to the kiddie gymnastics program.

At the Academy, the cadets rotated through a variety of different sports in their Physical Training sessions in the afternoons. They'd spend 4-6 weeks on lacrosse, then move on to soccer. When it got colder, they started indoor sports like squash or basketball or boxing or… gymnastics. The Academy liked sports that developed reaction times; after all, one of the military Academies' objectives was to produce fighters. Some people thought they didn't spend enough time at any one sport to really develop a skill and that was probably true. Ell performed well, but not spectacularly at those sports.

At this point, by working on her control, she was able to go into her own little version of the zone any time she wanted or needed her ability. More importantly, she could almost always keep herself out of the zone unless her stress levels were very high. She could even control how deep she went into the zone.

Nonetheless, she still found herself slipping into the zone when truly frightened or angry. The world still slowed down, her pulse became a loud, slow throb in her ears. Other sounds became distant and her control-coordination, already much better than most people's, became phenomenal.

After the incident where she'd laid out Sergeant Mason, she'd worked even harder at controlling her speed when she was in the zone so as not to be seen as a freak. Yet, while she was in the zone, it was difficult to tell what would be possible for others, or even for herself in her normal state. Fearful of being recognized as an aberrant monster of some kind, she pulled her punches, so to speak, purposefully and carefully underperforming if she slipped into the zone in order to keep from calling unwanted attention to herself. In order to do this, she'd developed the strategy of carefully watching the other cadets' execution of whatever new physical endeavor was called for and—if or when she slipped into the zone—carefully used her ability to perform almost exactly, or only slightly better than the normal abilities she'd just observed.

However, Ell's gymnastic rotation started with a video demonstration of a basic, relatively simple routine of moves on the uneven bars, performed by an Olympic caliber gymnast. The moves were shown at regular speed and then in slow-mo to clarify what was happening and how. Of course such an expert made those moves *appear* easy. The instructor, like many of their PT instructors, had a bit of a sadistic streak. She enjoyed making it *look* easy with the video, then watching the cadets fail on something that they'd *thought* should be easy. Her tradition included volubly lowering her expectations to what this particular group of uncoordinated bumblers could reasonably be expected to learn. Maybe a few giant swings on the bars, a good round-off on the floor and perhaps a simple end over vault that landed feet first. By no means great expectations, but nonetheless, some improvement in physical agility and well worth its while for the average cadet.

Unfortunately, Lieutenant Mabry looked over her clipboard and said, "Donsaii, up and at 'em. Let's see what you can do." Ell felt shock course through her as she realized that she was going to be the first one called upon to undertake their group's gymnastic routine!

Ell had frozen so Mabry bellowed, "Donsaii, you here?"

"Yes Ma'am." Ell stood and walked to the bars, trying to remain calm so that she could simply perform at her own normal level of coordination. The uneven bars routine had looked easy on the video, but she frantically wondered how another cadet would perform on it. Was this more difficult than it appeared? Her anxiety level rapidly escalated at being first—and in the spotlight—without any guidance on *how* to perform. At the focus of so much attention, she couldn't seem to stay out of the zone. She realized she was having serious stage fright, but couldn't seem to tamp it down. While she powdered her hands her heart started to pound, but then it seemed to slow down as the whole world slowed down.

She knew it was a bad sign when her heart sped up, then *seemed* to slow back down.

~~~

Lieutenant Mabry's intention was for the cadets to try the mount, which was in fact not a high difficulty
~~~

mount. Nonetheless, with no guidance, seldom did a cadet actually mount the bar, much less accomplish the second move in the routine. She had, however, shown a video of a complete, though simple routine on the uneven bars. Even though it was a low difficulty mount, the mount alone would be highly frustrating for the bunch of fully grown, non-gymnasts Mabry was supposed to have in her class. This was guaranteed to produce amazing and hilarious pratfalls on their attempt. As she stepped up to spot for that expected fall, Mabry looked forward to deriding the cadet's coordination.

~~~

That said, Ell didn't comprehend her instructor's Machiavellian plan. She'd been shown a full speed, then slow motion video of an apparently easy routine. She had *no* idea that the gymnast she'd been watching on the vid won a gold medal in the last Olympics. Then without an opportunity to realize that most of her classmates wouldn't even be able to mount the bars, she was called to the front of the class to try it—while she was deep in her zone due to her anxiety over being singled out first. By now her pulse throbbed very slowly in her ears.

She paused, hoping to damp down her zone. Mabry yelled, "What are you waiting for? The bars won't come to Mohammed!" In what seemed like *very* slow motion to Ell, she ran a few steps, bounced on the mounting springboard, and leapt up to grasp the high bar. She intentionally over extended her hips *well* beyond what the video demonstration had shown.

She kipped, kicking her legs up into flexion and then kicking them back, thrusting herself up to an arms
~~~

extended position, hips against and shoulders above the bar. Deep in the zone, this felt very, *very* easy. Her movements felt like they were in slow motion, so she carefully positioned herself in significantly more flexion than had been demonstrated in the video.

She thrust her hips against the bar and kicked up to a handstand on the bar. She made the handstand shaky and wavery, pretending she could barely balance on the bar and hoping that she wasn't overdoing her apparently poor coordination.

The Lieutenant hadn't said anything so far, so she dropped back, swung under and up on the other side of the bar to the next handstand.

She swung back down, released for the demonstrated transfer to the lower bar and *continued on to perform the entire simple routine that had been demonstrated on the video... including the dismount.*

The entire time Ell continued to perform markedly below her capability, placing her hands differently than she'd seen in the video, making unsteady, bobbling handstands, moving off center on the bars, and bending her knees unlike the demonstration. She purposefully fell down on the dismount.

She had no idea that the mistakes she purposely made, which seemed like gross clumsiness to her, were actually relatively minor and wouldn't have cost many points in a college competition.

~~~

Joy was in the class and told Phil about it later. "So Lt. Mabry's spotting for her to fall on the mount like the rest of us eventually did, but Ell just whips on by and does the whole routine! Mabry's standing there with her mouth hanging open, then getting more and more
~~~

pissed.

"By the time Ell falls down at the end, Mabry's red in the face. She's looking down at her clipboard, then she looks up at Ell and bellows. 'Cayydet!' she looks down at Ell's nametag, 'Donsaii, is it?'

"'Yes ma'am?'

"'The info you filled out at the beginning of this semester didn't say anything about you being a gymnast! If it did, you wouldn't *be* in this class! Did you think you could just slip in an easy grade this way?'

"Ell gets a real meek, 'I screwed up' look on her face and says 'No Ma'am.'

"Mabry says, 'How many years of gymnastics have you had?'

"And Ell, timid as can be, says, 'Two years Ma'am.'"

~~~

Ell carefully avoided telling anyone how old she'd been when she took those two years.

Mabry was one of the coaches for the Academy's gymnastics team and two years or no two years, once she got over her tiff, she realized she had a potentially excellent gymnast on her hands. She quickly apologized, then started proselytizing Ell to try out for the team. There were a lot of benefits to being on a team at the Academy, especially for doolies, not least of which was a chance to eat at the training tables and not spend your meals sitting at attention.

Ell gave a lot of thought to her resolution to avoid sports and focus on academics. Eventually, she decided that, during her freshman year, the benefits outweighed the costs. Therefore, when they announced a sign up for walk-ons, to various sports including gymnastics, would be held in the dining hall after the
~~~

evening meal, Ell went to the gymnastics team table. Two first class (senior) cadets staffed the table, talking earnestly to one another. Ell arrived and stood at attention for a couple of minutes before one deigned to look up at her and, with irritation, say, "What?"

Ell looked down, saw the cadet's name was Korsov and said, "Cadet Korsov, I would like to try out for women's gymnastics Ma'am."

Korsov looked her up and down and said, "You're pretty big. How much gymnastic experience do you have?"

"Just two years Ma'am."

"Oh, come on, Ms." she looked down at Ell's nametag, "Donsaii, is it?"

"Yes Ma'am."

"We're not asking just anyone who *feels* like it to apply. You need to have a realistic chance of competing at the collegiate level!"

Ell focused on the wall behind Korsov, "Yes Ma'am, I believe I do Ma'am."

"Really?" Korsov said drolly.

Ell continued looking straight ahead, "Yes Ma'am."

"Well, port me your name and info. I'll get you put on the list for the tryout tomorrow at 1600, but you'd *better* not be wasting our time."

"No Ma'am." Ell had Allan send her info to Korsov's AI. Once she'd been dismissed, she headed back to her room.

The next morning she received a posting to the gymnastics tryouts. It specified the gear she should dress in and provided an excuse to relieve her from other duties. She arrived at the gym just before 4PM and was able to watch some of the current gymnasts working on their routines before her tryout. Korsov, tiny like most gymnasts, shook her head when Ell arrived, but she and another senior level cadet took Ell and two other walk on hopefuls over to the floor exercise mat. They simply said, "Show us what you can do." Ell hung back and jockeyed carefully to place the other two doolie girls in front of her so they'd go first. She watched them tumble across the mat, doing hand springs and a few dance moves. They weren't as good as some of the college gymnastic videos Ell had watched the night before. One did do a double backflip, but she landed it badly.

When Ell's turn came she was irritated to notice that Cadet Korsov wasn't even watching her. She'd focused on one of the team's gymnasts on the bars across the room. The other senior cadet, name unknown to Ell, waved for her to go ahead, so she stepped out onto the mat, just slightly into the zone. Ell carefully scaled her performance, much of it consisting of elements she'd watched on video but never performed, to be just a little better than the routine of the team's gymnast who'd been practicing her floor exercise when Ell came into the gym. However, it was *far* better than the performances of the two other walk-ons. She finished back in the corner she had started from and found Korsov glaring at her.

Korsov looked down at her e-slate. "Two years?!"

"Yes Ma'am."

Korsov and the other senior cadet looked at one another, then Korsov said, "That's gotta be complete bullshit!" But, after a moment she shrugged, "I guess you can walk the walk, you're on the team." She glanced at the other two girls and shook her head. Their shoulders drooped as they headed for the exit.

~~~

Once on the team, Ell spent much of her first couple of weeks trying to gauge how good she could safely be without attracting inordinate attention. Once she'd figured that out, her stress level dropped so that she lost the tendency to go into the zone every time she was called on.

She only zoned when she actually wanted to.

At first Ell watched the other gymnasts on the team and carefully performed just a little better than the worst girls on the team. After a while she allowed her level of performance to gradually build until she was the number five member by the time they started competing in meets. That was all the higher she wanted to go. She'd only gone that high because it moved the irritating Korsov down to number six. She intended to continue competing at that level for the rest of the season.

Then, at the team's first meet, she got caught up in team spirit.

~~~

She'd missed the team's first meet—a real shellacking by BYU—because she'd had the flu. Therefore, Ell's first actual competition was against Navy, a high-pressure Academy rival. BYU'd had a bigger and significantly better team, but Navy was more their size and the Air Force was anxious to get a win. Ell's scores were good, but not extraordinary on the first routine. The same was true on the floor exercise, but the competition was wrapping up and Air Force was just a little behind. As she came to the vault the team started rabidly cheering her on, hoping for a good score to give them a little catch up. Courtney, the team captain, came up to whisper in her ear. "Stay calm and just do the best you can, a good score on this could pull us even." A little too excited with all the team fervor, Ell decided to do one vault at a pretty high level. She purposefully dropped mildly into the zone as she began her run. The world slowed, her stride achieved great precision, she hit the board like a small explosion, then fired off the table into a Yurchenko double with a twist, holding back only moderately from a maximum effort. She stuck her landing, but made it look like she might have to take a step by wavering a moment after she landed.

The judges were stunned and the audience began cheering wildly. Her vault had been nearly flawless and the height and distance were excellent. Ell's score didn't just bring the team up to a tie but actually gave them a slight lead. Her teammates were so ecstatic, Ell gave in to temptation and decided to push it some on the beam too. She didn't try to do anything special or highly difficult; she just inserted smaller bobbles than she usually did and stuck the landing with only a slight waver instead of her usual step.

Again the crowd went wild.

Linza, one of the other doolie gymnasts ran up to hug Ell, "That routine was awesome!" Linza hadn't personally ever witnessed an entire routine performed with only minor bobbles. "No sways to center, no hand waving? You made it look like the beam was two feet wide!" Ell's routine wasn't of great difficulty, so once again she didn't get an extremely high score. Nonetheless, its near perfection had the judges looking at each other in wonder.

Her score on beam had the fewest deductions of the meet.

~~~

The gymnastics coaches didn't miss the significance of these events and suddenly began thinking of Ell Donsaii in a whole new light. Could she be pushed to even higher levels? Were more of these near flawless performances available? Could she hit flawless with more difficult routines?

The answers to these questions were all yes—*if* the team really needed such a performance at a meet. This happened at more and more meets and Ell Donsaii slowly became a dark horse on the American gymnastics scene. Some began to wonder if this sudden apparition from nowhere was good enough for the Olympics that summer. Established athletes and their coaches were vehemently opposed to such an inexperienced and *old* gymnast even getting a *trial* for the Olympic squad which usually was made up of pre-college girls. If those detractors found out that, despite being halfway through her freshman year of college, she was actually only sixteen they were stunned.

Back at the Academy there were complaints that she couldn't train for the Olympics and still keep up with her duties.

Coach Mabry had long since gotten over her peeve to become Ell's greatest supporter. Mabry began pulling every string she could to ensure that Ell would be allowed to try out.

***

Three days later Jamal came home to find his light on again. For a moment he wondered again how the man had gotten in, but it seemed unimportant in the
~~~

grand scheme of things. Jamal coded open his door and walked over to where the man sat.

It was the same man. "Well?" was all he said.

Jamal picked up his slate from the coffee table and opened it to the news page showing the wreck on the freeway. It had been attributed to youthful vandals who "would not have understood the terrible thing they were doing." Jamal had been horrified to find out that a young woman had been driving the van. She and her father, who sat in the seat behind her, had both been killed by the concrete block. The young woman's son in the other back seat had been unharmed.

But orphaned.

Realizing that he'd slaughtered a mother and grandfather in front of their young son had produced a *déjà vu* that sent Jamal reeling into the bathroom to throw up. The irony that killing a mother and grandfather was exactly what had been done to *him* overwhelmed Jamal. He'd skipped classes that day and considered killing himself in atonement.

He hadn't had the courage.

"Here," he said, handing the news story to the man.

The man peered quizzically at the slate. Jamal suddenly realized the man's command of written English was poor. "The automobile wreck there. I caused it. Two Americans were killed."

The man looked back down at the pictures, then back up at Jamal. "Chickenshit! Couldn't look them in the eye I suppose."

"I didn't want to get caught. The investment made in me would have been wasted."

The man looked at Jamal like a particularly undesirable specimen of insect. "Yes, of course." He grunted, "Well, you need more training it seems.

Tickets will be delivered. You will spend the first part of the summer in a training camp. But for now you must make reservations to go to Dallas at the end of the summer."

"What's in Dallas and when should I be there?"

Another grunt, "The Olympic games. Arrange to be there two weeks before and for the duration of the competitions."

***

Ell's AI notified her that she was excused from her 10 o'clock class to report to the Academy Commandant's office. The notification didn't say why, so she was pretty nervous when she knocked on the doorframe. "Cadet Donsaii reporting as ordered, sir."

"Come."

Ell stepped inside and saw Coach Mabry and the gymnastics head coach in the office with the Commandant. Her heart fluttered, wondering if maybe someone had decided her gymnastic performances were outside the realm of possible. She came to attention and saluted.

The commandant studied her, "Ms. Donsaii, your coaches want you to be able to try out for the Olympic team... What do you think about this opportunity?"

"Sir, it's likely I'm too old and inexperienced to succeed."

"But, you'd like to try?"

After a long pause she quietly said, "Yes sir."

"How are you going to keep up with the curriculum while you're gallivanting off to trials, and then possibly spending time at the Olympic Team training camp and perhaps even participating in the Olympics?"

"Sir, I believe I can keep up."

Coach Mabry stepped up. "Commandant, if I may interject?"

"Go ahead Coach."

"I can forward Cadet Donsaii's transcript to your AI sir, but if you will take my word for it, the cadet tested out of so much of the curriculum that she's almost two years ahead of the typical freshman."

The commandant's eyebrows rose. "So you're telling me that she could miss or fail *all* her classes this semester and still graduate on time?"

"Yes sir."

"And there's also a..." the commandant looked up at his HUD, "Cadet Zabrisk, a wrestler who might make an Olympic team?" Ell was startled, this was the first she'd heard of that possibility. She felt surprised that Phil hadn't been bragging about it.

"Yes sir, I understand he's also a little ahead of the curriculum. Also, I believe the wrestlers aren't expected to show up at the Olympic team training facility until shortly before the Games. He can remain here at the academy until just about six weeks before the actual Olympics. We would only need to grant him an exception to a part of the summer training schedule."

"Hmmm," the Commandant leaned back and stared into the distance, "well it doesn't seem like this is going to happen very often. I suppose we can bend a few rules to let them try out. If they make the teams, maybe we'll just have to bend a few more."

Ell's heart lifted, though she wasn't quite sure why she wanted to go to the Olympics. "Thank you, sir."

***

Phil was actually having a hard time *not* bragging about his Olympic prospects. At first the natural reluctance of doolies to have a spotlight shining on them, thus acting as a lightning rod for upperclassmen's harassment inhibited him. Also he'd been admiring Ell for her humility in the face of his increasing realization of her astonishing capabilities. He could hardly brag about himself, and at the same time admire her lack of hubris. So when he received word that he'd been selected for the Olympic team, he actually kept it to himself! Even more to his own amazement, when word got out that he was on the team, he managed to downplay it! "I just got lucky in a few meets." This went over great with the 22nd squadron's upperclassmen who, rather than harassing him as he'd expected, took great pride in having an Olympian in their squadron and bragged about him to upperclassmen in other squadrons.

Phil was basking in that pride when Joy whispered from behind him as they waited in formation, "Phil, did you hear that Ell's going too?"

"Going where?"

"The Olympics, doofus."

Phil was nonplussed a moment. Did Joy mean that Ell was going to be going with an Academy contingent sent to cheer for him? He hadn't heard of any plans to send a group. Then his hairs prickled yet again. He knew she was on the gymnastics team and was supposed to be pretty good. No one had said anything to him about *how* good, though he knew she'd been credited with helping the team win some meets. It couldn't be that she was actually *in* the Olympics could it? He grunted noncommittally.

"Yeah," Denson said, "pretty amazing, huh? Did you know that the last Olympic athlete from the Academy was decades ago? How awesome is it that there're not only two Olympic athletes coming from the Academy this year, but that they're both from the same squadron!"

Phil felt like someone had kicked him.

It just seemed that for *everything* Phil was good at, Ell was either just as good, or worse, outshone him!

Chapter Five

Ell arrived at the Olympic training camp with mixed feelings. She'd decided that she loved the thought of being an Olympic athlete. Kristen and Gram called almost every day, beside themselves with excitement. The Academy'd decided that the PR value of her Olympic status justified sending a couple of instructors with her to training camp and then on to the Olympics. The instructors were there to help her keep up with her curriculum, hopefully allowing her to remain far in advance of the other cadets in her year.

Ell's gymnastics performances so far had been labeled uneven. Her performances at the Olympic trials had been more than good enough to put her on the team, but Lieutenant Mabry and Olympic Head Coach Benson were concerned about how often she followed unbelievably good routines by muffing simple moves.

Ell's mixed feelings resulted partially from the coaches' obvious stress over her questionable capabilities, but more from that fact that the other girls on the team had known each other—and many had been together at training facilities—for several years. They were all the physically tiny type that usually won Olympic medals. In fact this year *all* of them were still in high school. In addition, Ell knew that she'd displaced a popular gymnast whom they'd all enjoyed having on their team with them.

Despite her excellent performance in the trials Ell was listed as an alternate because she'd performed poorly in a meet right before the trials. A meet in which her team didn't need the points. So, no one was sure how she'd fit into the team or whether she'd perform well when it counted. They would only put her on the official team if she could demonstrate consistency.

Ell'd convinced herself that she shouldn't expect major problems fitting in, but troubles were waiting for her when she first walked in with Head Coach Benson.

"Girls," the coach shouted to the room in general. The girls in the room stopped what they were doing. "This is Ell Donsaii." The coach introduced her in a pleasant tone but the nine other gymnasts at the camp all simply stared at her, many with their arms folded unhappily in front of them.

Ell realized that, while these young women knew that they wouldn't all go to the Olympics, they'd expected to lose out to one of their own, not to a newcomer. She smiled brightly and gave a little wave, "Hi!"

No one said anything in return, though a few waved perfunctorily. After a moment they all turned back to their equipment. Coach Benson quietly said, "They'll get over their snit after a while. Just be friendly." Then she led Ell over to the vault and said, "Let's see what you can do."

That evening Ell found out that all the other girls were paired up with roommates.

She had a room to herself.

Ell had organized her room and put away all her stuff. She was about to start studying when there was a knock at her door. When she opened it one of the assistant coaches was there. "Aren't you coming to dinner?"

"Oh, I *am* hungry! But I didn't know anything about how meals are arranged here."

"None of the girls told you how to have your AI access our schedule on the Net?"

"Um, no." Ell felt nonplussed at the thought that they would have helped her with that after completely ignoring her the entire practice. "If you don't mind showing me, that'd be great."

"Okay, but let's do it on the walk over or you'll miss the entire meal."

"Thanks, Coach Baiul."

Baiul's AI gave Ell's a link as soon as they started over. When they got to the little dining hall, all the other girls were sitting at one big table and nearly done with dinner. Ell wound up sitting with her two instructors from the Academy as well as Coach Baiul and some of the other teachers.

***

Days, then weeks, passed without much change in the frosty attitude of the other gymnasts. Ell tried to make friends with the other girls, but they iced her out. The team's vault specialist, Anna Kernova, seemed especially antagonistic. Coach Baiul asked Anna to spot for Ell once while the coach ran to the bathroom. Anna rolled her eyes and with a curled lip, said, "You're *way* too big for me to spot. We'll just have to wait."

While they waited Ell tried the gambit of asking Anna for advice, "Do you have any suggestions on how I could stick my landings a little better?"

Anna looked up at Ell with an incredulous

expression, "Really?!" Then she turned back to studying the vault runway, arms crossed over her chest.

Ell wondered what Anna had meant with the "Really?" *Did she think it preposterous that I'd ask her for help? Or unimaginable that she'd give any? Or pitiful that I'd try to act friendly?*

It seemed likely that Anna disliked Ell because Anna's vault specialty was where Ell performed the best and most consistently. Vault didn't really take stamina like some of the other routines that were long enough to wear into Ell's limited endurance. Ell'd read up and decided she must have a very high percentage of fast twitch muscle. The power and speed of fast twitch muscle would at least partially explain how she had the quickness to do the surprising things she could do. But fast twitch muscle fibers provided little endurance.

Even without going in the zone, Ell could actually do the most difficult vaults perfectly, over and over, though she carefully made at least minor mistakes on every one to keep suspicions down. By the end of a floor exercise Ell was tired enough that mistakes were, if not inevitable, certainly easy to make.

Anna called Ell, "Ms. Donsaii." At first Ell wondered why, but then realized that Anna thought that Ell was nineteen or twenty like most rising college sophomores. Anna was fifteen and would turn 16 during the calendar year of this Olympics, the very youngest you could be and still be allowed to compete. Ell thought about telling Anna that she was only sixteen (well sixteen and a half), but she'd worked so hard to keep her young age secret she decided against it. Not only because she'd been *told* to keep it a secret, but also so that she wouldn't be treated differently by her classmates at the Academy. The fact that she'd been given a special waiver for her age made the staff at the Academy especially sensitive to helping her keep the secret.

Ell tried to deal with her unfriendly reception by being relentlessly cheerful and helping the other girls whenever she could. She clapped for them when they did well and complimented them for good moves.

Her friendliness made little headway. The other gymnasts never returned any favors unless the coaches badgered them into it. Sometimes she saw some of them, heads together in heated discussion, throw angry looks her way.

~~~

Lieutenant Mabry, one of Ell's two instructors from the Academy, was *supposed* to be helping her keep up with her Academy curriculum. But that didn't seem to be her major focus. "Donsaii! What the hell were you doing out there today?"

"Ma'am?" Ell wondered what this was about. Mabry badgered her constantly about her gymnastics performances. She wasn't supposed to be coaching Ell for gymnastics, they had the Olympic coaches for that. But Mabry had been in gymnastics her whole life and came to every practice, to "observe." Daily, during Ell's supposed study time, she made suggestions on how Ell could have done better in this or that gymnastic routine.

"Your vaults! They were terrible! What the hell were you thinking about? I *know* you can do better than that!"

Ell knew it too. She'd fluffed those vaults on purpose so she could try asking Anna's advice one more time. Anna'd been a little less standoffish that day, and, once again, Ell had been looking for something that might let
~~~

them to become friends.

Anna had given her the usual cold shoulder though. To Mabry she said, “Just had an off day Ma’am.”

“I’ll say! You’re so inconsistent I’ll be surprised if they don’t throw you off the team! They can’t afford to have someone who’s either really hot or *really* cold. Everyone knows you *can* turn in better performances than any of those girls, but they don’t know if you *will*. What if you turn cold at the big one? You *do* know that they’re only taking seven of the ten girls from this training camp to the actual Olympics don’t you?”

This sent a spike of dismay through Ell. She actually hadn’t been worried about her position on the team because *she* knew she could turn it on to produce a stunning performance if she needed to. She hadn’t considered the possibility that the coaches wouldn’t recognize that capability and therefore might just leave her at home. She resolved to stop fluffing any routines. It hadn’t been making her any friends anyway. From here on out, she’d perform better than almost anyone on the team *every* time so that she’d be guaranteed a spot on the team.

Friends or no.

Lonely or not.

***

That night as she lay awake, instead of pondering her extra dimension and quantum mechanics math, she worried about the possibility that she might be dropped from the team after all the effort she’d put in on it so far. She considered what she could do to *guarantee* herself a spot. She was thinking about how she could fine tune her Yurchenko two and a half twist when she had a flash of insight.

The Yurchenko vault was named after Soviet gymnast Natalia Yurchenko, the first gymnast to perform that particular vault. The two and a half twist starts with a round off from a sprint, the hands hit the spring board, the gymnast flips end over end, then strikes the vaulting table with her hands. From there she turns end over end one and a half more times with her body out straight in a layout position while also spinning on her longitudinal axis two and a half times. *Then* she lands on her feet! This was a high difficulty vault, but easy for Ell, even when she wasn't in the zone. Ell realized that, as easy as many of the high difficulty vaults were for her, when she was in the zone, she should be able to come up with some vaults that hadn't ever been performed before.

By *anyone*.

She slipped out of bed and quietly over to the gym. At two in the morning the gym stood as empty as she'd hoped. Despite all the times she'd been warned never to do gymnastics alone for fear of being hurt without a spotter, she lined up at the vault runway anyway. She considered and decided to try a Yurchenko *with two and a half* end over end rotations or saltos—instead of one and a half—as well as the usual two and a half twists.

She dropped deep into the zone as she flew down the runway and went into her round off.

Springboard.

Hit the table *much* harder than usual to get altitude.

Start to flip and twist hard!

Hah! She could feel she was actually going to flip end over a little more than two and a half rotations. Ell stretched her legs and arms as long as possible to slow her rotation.

She stuck her landing.

She did it one more time to work off the rough edges and the second one felt perfect. Good! That was one secret weapon she could pull out if they seemed to be thinking about not taking her to the Olympics.

She couldn't stay in the zone long enough to try anything else that night, but over the next few nights she snuck over to the gym and worked out other, never before performed moves for beam, bars and floor.

~~~

The next day Coach Benson intercepted Ell on her way to practice. "I want you to alternate vaults with Anna. You'd be our best vaulter except you blow your landing so often. After each of your vaults, wait by the landing zone long enough to watch Anna's landings. Anna's are consistently good and I want you to try to imprint what she does."

Ell simply said, "Yes ma'am." She headed for the vaulting runway. Bobbling the landing had been Ell's habit to that point in the training. It deflected attention from how perfect her vaults could be, *and* she hoped it'd help her make friends with Anna. Bobbling the take-off could be dangerous so she never underperformed that part of the routine. Ell dutifully watched Anna stick her landings. Then she went to perform her own vault and did her best to slightly under-replicate whatever small bobble Anna'd just made.

Coach Benson was standing by the landing area spotting for both of them and as Ell stood across from her the coach spoke steadily to Ell about how to improve her landings. As Ell improved her landings and
~~~

repeatedly stuck them better than Anna did, the Coach became enthusiastic about how well her idea was working. This made Ell nervous because the Coach didn't seem to be watching closely enough to help Anna if she made a bad landing. Admittedly, Anna seldom made bad landings.

As Anna made each sprint for her vaults, Ell tried to get Coach's attention focused back on spotting Anna. After all, Ell was *supposed* to be watching Anna's landings, so she'd turn to concentrate her own attention on Anna's vaults, despite the coach's continued lecturing.

Anna's hands struck the springboard with an odd sound!

Ell's panic reaction flooded through her as Anna flipped.

Then her hand skidded on the vaulting table.

Anna started tumbling through the air out of control!

Ell's zone crashed over her and her world slowed to a crawl. Ell saw Coach Benson stop talking and begin reacting. Ell noticed that Anna's eyes had opened wide in panic.

She'd gone rigidly into extension, slowing her rotation. Ell carefully considered Anna's trajectory and rotation—she was going to land head first. *Hard*!

Ell'd already crouched, now she thrust up into a leap, arm tackling Anna's upper body in order to slow Anna's rotation even further.

Ell absorbed a lot of Anna's rotation which made her begin to tumble herself.

Ell let go and spun her arms in a couple of violent windmills—though, deep in the zone, those windmilling motions seemed quite slow to her. The windmilling stopped Ell's rotation.

She again grabbed Anna by the arm and corrected Anna's tilt.

Ell and Anna slammed hard to the mat.

But, they landed feet first. Anna clung to Ell for a moment, gasped and shuddered once, then stiffened and quietly but emphatically, said, "I *don't* need *your* help, Donsaii."

Coach Benson gaped for a moment, then said, "That's not the standard and approved spotting method Ell... But it worked well enough I guess."

That night at dinner Ell sat down across from Anna in a vain hope that she might have softened her dislike.

Anna stared at her for a moment, then got up and moved to the other end of the table.

Ell sighed, it seemed she'd just as well stop trying to make friends and just do what she had to do in order to beat out the others for a spot on the official Olympic team. Hopefully, *without* using any of the secret elements she'd developed.

~~~

The next day Ell decided a good strategy might be to start doing as well as she could without going into the zone and let that take her to whatever level on the team it took her to. The first apparatus she'd been assigned to by the coaches that day happened to be vault again. Of course Anna was working on vault too, being the vault specialist. The entire team had participated in some warm-ups then started to their individual assignments. Ell arrived at the beginning of the vault runway just a little bit ahead of Anna but Anna stepped in front of Ell with a glare, "*I'm* going first!" Ell opened her hand toward the lane indicating she should
~~~

go ahead. Anna stepped up to her mark and looked down the lane with focused concentration. Ell expected her to go, but instead she turned to Ell and said, "Watch how this is done, ol' lady." Then she took a deep breath and started her sprint.

Ell, at a loss to understand why Anna despised her so, did watch Anna's vault, a very difficult double front half-out. Anna did it very well, with only a small step on her landing. Ell realized Anna'd probably chosen that vault because Ell hadn't ever done it.

Anna probably thought it was beyond Ell's capabilities.

Ell hesitated a moment then broke her resolution and let herself slip a bit into the zone. With the world slowed, she thought through exactly what Anna had just done and started down the sprint lane herself, letting herself go just a little faster than she usually did.

She launched a little harder off the vaulting table than usual and did a double front, half-out herself, sticking the landing as well as she could for her first time doing a vault and only being slightly in the zone.

This turned out to be very well indeed. Ell stuck a perfect landing several feet farther down the lane than Anna had.

Coach Baiul had been spotting for them and exclaimed, "Ell! I didn't know you could do a double front! That was perfect! Can you do it routinely?"

"I think so Ma'am." Ell saw Anna glaring at her. Anna did another vault while the coach was still talking to Ell so she and Anna walked back to the vault runway together.

Although Anna was ignoring Ell, Ell said quietly, "I'm not sure exactly why you hate me Anna, but if you want to teach me vaults, I guess I'll just have to learn them as well as I can."

Anna stared stonily ahead and didn't respond.

Ell immediately regretted the dig.

That wasn't the way she wanted to live her life.

***

Jamal ran from his tent to the firing line and brought the venerable AK-47 to his shoulder. He squeezed off three round bursts until it clicked on empty. Then after all the other trainees had finished firing he slogged through the sand to retrieve his target.

Hamid, his instructor, rubbed his crooked nose and clucked over the paper on which the outline of a head had been perforated in four locations. "Four hits out of an entire magazine." Hamid shook his head, "You should hope your life never depends on your shooting." Jamal wiped the sweat from his brow, but kept his eyes downcast. Hamid was a hard ass.

Jamal had already been beaten badly on several occasions at the training camp. Once for insubordination, and three more times for poor performance of a skill he'd been assigned to learn. Though intellectually dull, most of the trainees were better athletes than Jamal. "Go!" Hamid said, "You'll shoot more tomorrow."

As Jamal trudged back to one of the awnings he looked up at the burning sky. He was pretty sure the camp must be somewhere in Northern Sudan, but Jamal'd been blindfolded for part of the trip. If he fled he'd have a difficult time escaping the country. He had no money *and* they had his passport.

Thoughts of breaking with the organization once he

got back to America had begun crossing his mind more and more frequently.

Many of the other young men in the organization were religious fanatics, eager to sacrifice their own lives in Jihad. Though Jamal had felt the same ten years ago, his commitment had waned. When he brought the deaths of his family to mind, his rage would return, but his rage had been tempered by the fact that he'd committed almost exactly the same atrocity against a family himself. The other young men here wouldn't feel it was the same since the family he'd destroyed had been Christian. However, Jamal had seen happy pictures of them as a family in the news.

Christian or no, he knew what he'd done had been a terrible thing.

"Jamal Assad?"

Jamal looked up into the cold eyes of a man he hadn't seen before. Eyes so cold he felt a chill down his spine despite the burning hot day. "Yes."

"There are some here who doubt your commitment."

"No, no, I am committed!" Jamal heard a tremor in his voice. Had the man read Jamal's mind? This man, he felt certain, would kill him without a second thought if Jamal's commitment lacked.

The man pulled a large knife out of a sheath. Jamal felt his heart pounding in his chest.

The man gripped it by the blade...

And tossed it, hilt first, to Jamal.

Jamal's ears were ringing and his head so swimming with relief that he almost didn't hear the man's next words. "Give me your toe."

"Wha... what."

"The small toe will do. As a token of your

commitment."

For a moment Jamal thought he might throw up. Prickles ran down his spine and a faint ringing came in his ears, but then he knelt to take off his shoe and it passed. He slowly unlaced his boot, then pulled off his sock. Grasping the knife firmly, he placed it over the joint of his small toe and with a violent motion threw his whole body forward, forcing the knife blade to crunch through his own toe. The pain was lancing and excruciating, but he was grateful that the knife was sharp.

~~~

To his amazement, Jamal found himself assigned as one of the leaders of a team sent to terrorize the Olympics. Hamid of the crooked nose, who'd terrorized Jamal at training camp, was the actual leader.

Jamal served more as a guide to America, but the fact that they consulted him before every move made him *feel* like a leader. Before returning to Tucson he was questioned endlessly as they deliberated over possible targets. They considered and discarded a plan to bomb the Olympic stadium. "Bomb sniffing" had become quite the art in America, and even if they did successfully set one off, the audience would have many foreign nationals. It would likely kill some Muslims as well.

Although the dead would go to Allah as martyrs, it would create dissension amongst those who were weak in the faith.

Setting off a bomb elsewhere in Dallas would be easier and they could arrange it to be in an area where only infidels would be found. A Christian church seemed a good choice. This plan foundered on the desire to
~~~

devastate America in front of the worldwide audience of the Olympic contests. No, they decided they must kill Olympic athletes, preferably from the American team alone. Jamal searched on the internet and determined that the teams were to stay in housing dormitories away from the actual sports complex and would be bussed to the complex on a daily basis.

Jamal returned to Tucson, but then caught his flight to Dallas the next day. He arrived before any of the others. Using a false identity, he'd rented a Suburban SUV and rooms in a disreputable apartment building. He picked up two more martyrs at the airport and dropped them off at the apartments. Hamid and the other five members of the team were unable to get visas to enter the country legally. Hamid had emailed Jamal GPS coordinates and on a specified night Jamal let the truck's AI take him to a road near the specified location. Then he dutifully drove the SUV manually according to his AI's directions, first on a dirt road and then off even that road into the desert near the border with Mexico. He parked when he reached the specified coordinates, rolled down the windows and turned off the lights. At first he sat alertly, staring into the night, but eventually boredom set in. He reclined the seat back and dozed off.

Something cold bumped his ear and he woke to the realization that it was a gun muzzle! "Asshole." Hamid growled in garlicky Arabic. "I could have killed you! Wake up!"

"Sorry." Jamal said, rubbing his eyes and sitting up. The doors of the SUV opened and it rapidly filled with the six men. Several heavy boxes went into the back. Jamal's nose was assaulted by the smell of sweaty unwashed men. He started the vehicle and turned it around for the long drive back to Dallas.

Hamid sat in the passenger seat. “You have a place for us to stay?”

“Yes, in a slum, all the nice locations are full because of the Olympics.”

“We don’t need ‘nice.’” Hamid growled. ”Do you have American style clothing for us?”

“Some, but only one set each. We’ll need more, especially for the little guy.”

“Why?”

“Because, I didn’t know how big you guys are.”

“No, why do we need more than one set?”

“Because, in America you must be clean and your clothes must not stink. Smelling like you do, they’ll watch every move you make and you’ll get arrested just for existing, much less for committing any terrorism.”

Hamid grunted skeptically, but in the morning he showered and made the rest of the men do so as well. Then he helped Jamal shepherd them all down to a nearby thrift shop to pick up more clothes. Hamid and one other spoke English well. Two more spoke broken English, but could get by. The remaining four spoke only a few words.

They spent the day driving around Dallas and evaluating the lay of the land. A land of concrete and buildings and new sports stadiums. They saw where the athletes would be housed and where they would strive to win their medals. Arguments broke out over the likely routes to be taken from the dormitories to the arenas. They separated into small teams with an English speaker in each group. The teams rode in the city buses and took taxis so that each would understand how the city functioned.

It took considerable effort just to determine that the

buses the teams would ride in to and from the games were to be rented from companies that provided drivers. It would not be possible to know which bus would transport the American teams ahead of time.

Hamid massaged his deformed nose and said, "We'll just have to board the bus after the Americans are already on it."

Jamal felt his brow rising, "Board the bus, how? I thought we were going to put a bomb under it?"

"How will we do that when we don't even know which bus they'll be on? No, we'll kidnap them first and hold the city in terror under the threat of their deaths. We'll wait to actually kill them *until* the eyes of the entire world are upon us!"

"But, with the eyes of the world upon us, escape will be impossible!"

Hamid's eyes glittered, "Of course. We are *martyrs*! We'll do this deed in the *face* of death and they'll speak of us for all time!" He clapped Jamal on the shoulder, "Our time in *this* world is short my friend."

Jamal swallowed and looked around. The other men's eyes were fervent and if any of *them* were dismayed he didn't see it on their faces. Jamal's eyes shifted to the floor and he hoped they didn't hear his heart thumping in his chest. Distantly, he wondered when he'd become afraid to die. For years he'd told himself he stood ready to die for vengeance. Surprise washed over him to realize how little vengeance still pumped in his veins.

He'd *indeed* been seduced by the Great Satan.

With time and a great deal of argument a plan slowly gelled. They would wear athletic suits in the American Olympic team colors and would then wait along the route to the arenas. When they saw a bus full of Americans they'd stop that bus and board it, pretending to be American athletes who'd mistaken the boarding location. Then they would hijack the bus to a location where they could broadcast the killing of the athletes, preferably one by one, to the world.

A visit to a Wal-Mart equipped them each with athletic garments closely resembling the sweat suits of the American Olympic team. Then they started examining possible routes that buses might take between the dormitories and the stadiums. Jamal and Hamid, with one or two others at a time, drove the possible routes and up and down side streets, looking for a site where they could hold the athletes after they captured them. They had no idea what might work and argued vehemently over various possibilities. A large parking garage stood just off the main street to the arenas and Jamal turned into it. Hamid said, "What the hell are you doing?"

"This parking deck would be easy to drive a bus into. I thought we could check it out." Jamal drove up a wide ramp that circled, taking the Suburban higher and higher in the deck.

"But it's open to the outside! We'd have no protection from snipers!"

"At least let's drive to the top and look out at the city from up there. Who knows what we'll see."

Hamid crossed his arms and sat back into his seat, obviously unhappy. When they got to the top, they got out and the four of them wandered around looking off the top deck to see the city. Jamal had to admit he didn't see anything useful and Hamid soon complained, "*This* was a complete waste of time."

As they drove back down Jamal said, "Maybe one of these lower levels, we could park the bus near the perimeter of the deck..."

Hamid interrupted, "No! That's stupid. We need a completely enclosed space."

Jamal, distracted by Hamid's contempt, missed the street level exit and suddenly realized that the parking spiraled down below street level as well. "What about down here?"

Hamid merely grunted in doubt. The area below street level was closed off from the outside world and poorly lit, but still, attackers would be able to approach from many angles. But then they came to the bottom level where they found that a quarter of the total area of the lowest deck was walled off in concrete. The entrance to that section was an enormous rolling steel door that would be large enough to drive an entire bus through! They got out and examined it, it wasn't even locked! With all four of them heaving on it they were able to raise the door enough for Jamal and Hamid to slip under with flashlights. They found an enormous room. It was empty but for a few ladders, some cleaning supplies and an old pickup with a flat tire. Hamid asked, "What's this room for?"

Jamal, who had been wondering exactly the same thing, shrugged his shoulders. It seemed to be a waste of an enormous amount of valuable parking space. There was one human sized door, also sturdy steel, but no other openings. They wandered around examining the entire room. It didn't even have ventilation ducts or openings other than the doors, suggesting that it must have been designed for storage. There was a large grate in the floor near the back corner and the floor sloped toward it. At first Jamal wondered if they had intended to use it for washing vehicles, but there was no water spigot near it. The only spigot was across the room near the cleaning supplies. Then Jamal realized that water must leak into the deck and run down here during storms. That corner was the lowest point in the entire deck. The grate probably served as a storm drain which explained why it was so large.

The concrete walls of the underground room were sixteen inches thick and the steel doors would be very difficult to break through. Hamid proclaimed the room to be perfect and sent Jamal to get the other team members while he began planning.

When Jamal returned, Hamid told him to find plans on the web for the deck so that they could determine where the storm drain went. To his surprise Jamal found that he couldn't connect to the net down in the bottom of the deck. He had to drive back up almost to street level in order to get a signal. His AI then downloaded plans for the deck, but to his astonishment the available plans didn't show the storm drain at all! Instead, a sump pumping system was shown from that back corner of the deck, to pump back up about four feet to access the storm drain system. Jamal surmised that they hadn't been able to excavate quite as deeply as they had planned and so the floor level was above the storm system rather than below it as anticipated by the architect. At the slightly higher level it could drain directly into the storm system rather than requiring the pump. This he confirmed by looking at the plan for the entrance. The plan showed a level drive into the deck whereas they'd actually had to drive up a ramp about 4 feet to enter. The plans, at least the ones available on the net, didn't show changes they'd apparently made during construction.

The plans labeled the big room on the lowest level, "valuable car storage." Perhaps that part of the business plan had never borne fruit? With the entire team there, they were able to lift the large grate and one by one they climbed down into the storm system. At present it had only a small trickle of water. They walked along until they found an access pipe with rungs in its side that led up to a manhole cover.

They left Yousef at that manhole cover and Hamid and Jamal went back up to street level. They walked along where they thought the storm sewer ran, looking for manhole covers. When they found one, Hamid used the net to order Yousef to stick a wire up through the pick hole in the manhole cover. Nothing happened so they searched for another manhole cover closer to the deck. This time, when Yousef stuck the wire up they saw it. They had him go to the next access point and do it again, the third cover they came to exited into an alley. Hamid was delighted and began to talk of possible escape. "They'll *think* we have no way out! We'll get a welder, and weld those damn steel doors shut so it takes them forever to get in. Then we'll kill all the Americans, leave through the drain that they won't know about because it isn't on the damned net they rely on for everything. We'll come out here in this alley and disappear into the city!"

Jamal, heartened by the possibility that he might not die, became a little more enthusiastic himself.

Then Hamid angrily realized they couldn't connect wirelessly to the net from down in their "redoubt" as he was calling the concrete room at the bottom of the deck. That would make it very difficult to publicize their capture of the Olympians, their demands and the eventual killing of the athletes.

Hamid was delighted when Jamal told him that he

could hardwire a signal repeater up to the street level. A visit to an electronics shop provided the materials and then they drove back to the parking deck at two in the morning. Hamid barked orders as they strung the wire from the basement redoubt up to the ground level.

It became apparent to Jamal that Hamid planned to place the antenna on the roof of the parking deck. Worried, Jamal said, "But they'll be able to triangulate and find us almost immediately."

"What?"

"First they'll find the antenna where our signal enters the net. Then they'll come down to this area of town and search for the source with direction finders. If all our signals come directly from the top of the parking deck, they'll immediately search the deck and eventually its bottom levels for us."

"So?"

"So, when they find us they may do something that we don't expect. Maybe they'll think of something that'll stop us from completing our mission. It'd be good if they had a hard time finding us, then some time will pass before they get the opportunity to disrupt our plans."

"Okay then, where should the wire go?"

Jamal proposed that they string it across the street, piggybacked on one of the other wires that crossed to the next building, then to the top of that building and across to the other side of it. He had a few bad moments when it appeared that Hamid intended Jamal to personally string the wire, but then, Abdul, the small man, volunteered to do it. It seemed he had no fear of heights. He simply hung under the existing wires while crawling across like a monkey. Then he scaled the next building dragging the wire as if it were a completely ordinary task. On the way back he even fastened the antenna wire into place every few feet with cable ties while hanging high above the street.

~~~

Once they had their plan mostly in place they settled down to a few daily excursions to increase familiarity with the city. They bought a welder and practiced with it. They bought caulk to seal the doors against tear gas and they carefully caulked every crack they found in the concrete. Two large spotlights were purchased and tested to be sure that they could get good video and audio from their executions out onto the net. Hamid's plan involved making outrageous demands, then killing an Olympian every hour until he thought the Americans were about to blow their way into the redoubt. Then they'd kill the remainder of the athletes and make their escape while a long prerecorded diatribe was being broadcast on the net to distract the police. "Yousef will remain on the outside to watch what the police are doing and keep us informed so that we'll know when and what to do."

Jamal said angrily, "Why Yousef? I know the city better."

Hamid looked at Jamal with suspicion, "Because Yousef looks like one of the Hispanics that are so plentiful here. Why do you want to remain outside?" His eyes narrowed further, "Is Jamal, chicken?"

Jamal said nothing for a moment, then swallowed, "No, I just think I can do a better job."

Yousef smirked. "Chicken," he stage whispered.

~~~

Yousef bought binoculars and rented an office in the

building across the street from the parking deck. It had a window looking over the entrance to the deck. On another late night they strung another hardwire down to the redoubt from Yousef's new office, this time for a simple two way intercom that Yousef would use to communicate with Hamid, even if net access had been cut off.

They had a couple of celebratory feasts, congratulating each other on deeds to be done and praying over their last days here on earth in case they did not succeed with their escape. All of them were required to watch as many news feeds as possible about the American Olympic athletes so that they'd recognize them.

Jamal found himself intrigued by a particularly striking woman gymnast named Donsaii…

Chapter Six

Ell walked into the glaring lights of Olympic Stadium in Dallas like a spectator. Performing consistently at a high level, she'd been accepted onto the official seven person team without having to use any of her secret moves. She felt ecstatic to be there at the Olympics. Her head swiveled every which way as she strode along in the middle of the group of American athletes. Intermittently she bounded up and down with her enthusiasm. The other young female gymnasts energetically bounced around her like pinballs.

When the team got to their place in the center of the field, Ell wandered through the Americans looking for Phil. To her surprise she was stopped by a couple of the swimmers who wanted her autograph! Though she'd seen a videography team at the gymnastics training camp and her mother had told her about a news special on the net concerning the gymnastics team, she had no idea that she'd been singled out as a dark horse, and featured large in the news reports. The general public found her fascinating, partly because of her looks, but also in large part because video of her astonishingly perfect routines were run in comparison to some bad landings and routines that were interesting only in that Ell hadn't been hurt! The story of her late entry to gymnastics, her young age to be in college, and her military cadet status interested Olympic fans too. As usual, women's gymnastics was one of the most popular attractions of the Olympics. This in combination with Ell's looks brought such attention that she'd gradually become one of the best known athletes of this Olympics. She had both passionate supporters who rooted for her and vehement detractors who were sure she'd flop in real competition.

"Sure, I'd be honored." Ell said to the autograph seeking swimmers. She noticed that one of the swimmers had a large stack of autograph cards. "Can I bum some of your cards to get some autographs of my own?" They were happy to share and she started with the two swimmers' autographs and moved on, looking for Phil. She ran into Michael Fentis, the sprinter, who appeared bored with the entire event. He'd been winning gold medals on the world stage for quite some time, so she realized this probably wasn't that big a deal to him. Ell strode up to him and said, "Mr. Fentis, might I obtain your autograph?"

Fentis didn't even glance at her, "No."

Ell was startled by his rudeness, but shrugged and went on. She asked all the athletes she recognized for autographs and they all graciously signed her cards, many asking her to return the favor. Then she saw a familiar broad back and blond head, "Phil!"

~~~

He turned, "Hey Ell!"

"Go 22nd Raptors!"

"Yeah! Raptors!" Phil found himself genuinely glad to see her and was bemused at the joy he felt when she threw her arms around him and gave him a fierce hug. He realized any resentment he'd felt toward her had finally dissipated. He'd been actively following news
~~~

about her gymnastics on the net and taking a lot of pride in her surprising talent. He'd become very proud to know her and called her a friend when speaking of her to others.

Ell let go of Phil and bounced up and down exuberantly. "Isn't this great!"

Phil grinned back at her happy enthusiasm. "Yeah. Your first event is tomorrow?" He knew it was, he probably knew her schedule better than his own.

"Yup. But in the morning, so I'll be over to root you on in the afternoon. You kick some ass and make me proud, hear?"

"You bet!"

"Hey! I need your autograph!" she held out a card and a pen.

"Really?" he said taking them.

She turned her back so he could sign on her shoulder. "Of course! I want to show all my friends that I really did know ya. Write, 'To Ell Donsaii, signed in Olympic Stadium.'"

"Have you really been getting autographs?"

"Sure, except Michael Fentis. He was a real jerk about it. Maybe you could twist him into a pretzel for me?"

His brow wrinkled, "Why didn't you just hit him with your purse, kick him in the nuts and put him in the hospital?"

"Oh!" Ell put her hand over her mouth at the little exclamation she'd just let out. "Will you *ever* forgive me? I really *am* sorry." The crinkles around her eyes said she wasn't *too* sorry.

"Yeah... Hell..." Phil laughed. "I *deserved* it."

~~~
~~~

The next morning the gymnastics team, all wearing their brand new red, white and blue sweats, went out to catch the early bus to the arena. Coach Benson wanted them to get in some warm-ups before the actual competition started. Ell knew that it would be better for her to rest, as her biggest enemy was fatigue, but she was too wired to sleep in anyway. After they pulled out of the gate of the athletes' housing complex, she rested her head against the window of the bus to watch the city go by. She was startled to see a small group of people wearing Team USA sweats standing at one of the corners. She decided that they must be fans, but they were arguing with one another and didn't even seem to notice the bus going by.

In the gym, Ell commandeered a corner where she pretended to stretch but mostly tried to be unobtrusive in order to avoid the coaches' attention. Nonetheless Benson found her and dragged her over to the vault, "This is your best event, Ell. You should do a few to stick them into your motor memory."

"Yes sir." Ell said, repressing the sigh that nearly escaped. She did one vault, making sure Coach Benson was watching. She suppressed the zone, but did an excellent vault so Benson wouldn't demand that Ell do it over, then snuck back to her corner.

She'd been thinking about it and had decided that the Olympics would be her last gymnastics competition. Next year she wanted to get back to focusing on academics. Sitting at the training tables wouldn't be nearly as important once she was a cadet third class. After all, she'd refused to take an athletic scholarship for college *because* she wanted to focus on physics and engineering. Therefore she contemplated doing at least some of the events as well as she possibly could.

Would it cause trouble?

Her mother and grandmother had flown into Dallas three days before. The owner of the diner where Kristen still worked summers had become one of Ell's biggest fans and had given her mother time off with pay, though of course she was forgoing her tips. One of the Team USA Olympic sponsors had sprung for airline tickets for the two of them and put them up in a nice hotel. Ell had been able to go out to dinner with her Mom and Grandma the night before the lighting of the flame. Jake, of course, hadn't come to Dallas, though her mother claimed he had become quite proud of his stepdaughter and watched all the news feeds about Ell. He might have changed his attitude, but Ell still couldn't imagine liking him.

Since Ell'd broken Jake's arm, she and her mother had had several long discussions and Kristen now understood something about Ell's strange abilities. She'd told Ell how she had always wondered how Ell had so handily overcome Kristen's assailant when she was only eleven. In reality, Kristen was a little freaked out by the whole thing.

They'd talked at length about Ell's gifts as they related to the Olympics. Both of them were concerned that perhaps her strange talents in the zone should be kept secret for fear of people reacting badly to something they didn't understand. On the other hand they wondered whether, if she *didn't* use her talents, she might always regret *not* actually seeing just what she could do against the best in the world. How could she pass up this chance to see how she *really* compared? After agonizing about it she'd decided that she'd never know what could have been if she didn't do at least one event as well as she possibly could. Since she was starting on vault she'd decided to go full out on her first vault. No one paid much attention to first events anyway. She'd be able to see what was possible without too much risk.

When she was called for the vault she felt the butterflies coming and only suppressed them a little as she walked over to the runway. She stepped up to her mark and let the rush of the zone flood over her. With a little tremor she decided to go ahead with one of the secret weapons no one had ever seen. She threw her arms high and dropped her center of gravity to begin her run, the low throb of each foot strike thundering through her as she flew down the runway, then skipped into her round-off. *Deep* into the zone, she seemed to have forever to align her hands so that they struck the springboard together, exactly in the center. She hit with just the amount of resilience in her arms that she knew from hundreds of practice sessions would launch her perfectly to the table. Spin over once, still deep in zone's slow motion, allowing her to place her hands perfectly in the center of the table also. Thrust *hard*, up off the table into the air for *two and a half* rotations in layout, with two and a half twists as well! Because no one had ever done such a vault before, she knew it was going to cause problems for the judges. While turning, she realized that, this deep in the zone, she had thrust herself higher in the air than she'd ever been in a vault before. Despite all the spinning and twisting, the world flowed slowly enough beneath her that she could determine that she was perfectly centered in the lane. She noted that her rotation was slightly too fast and stretched her body more to slow it. Then she stuck her landing, exactly centered between the lines, perfectly balanced over feet that struck side by side as a single unit. She flexed her knees *just* enough to absorb the energy and keep from bouncing, then stood back up, throwing her arms up high and wide. She smiled broadly at the judges, knowing in her heart that she had just *perfectly* executed a vault that *no one* had even thought was possible before now!

Ell let the zone go and the rest of the world gradually came up to her speed. As she turned from her landing her eyes passed over the round eyed judges. As she came back down to earth she heard a roaring noise and turned to see people leaping to their feet, cheering wildly, shaking fists. She looked around to see if something had happened, but even the girls waiting to do other events were staring over at the vault section in general and her in particular.

~~~

Phil'd had Chuck notify him when Ell started her first Olympic routine and he watched it live on his HUD. He hadn't actually watched her before, and hadn't really seen many gymnastic events at all. In fact, he didn't really understand the vault and wondered, as she started down the runway, just what she was going to do. Or was supposed to do for that matter. The first thing he noticed was that she seemed to be running really fast. He wondered if it was a video artifact, but then Radin Venta, one of the gymnastics announcers said, "My God! Look at her go! I've never seen a vaulter sprint this fast. Will she be able to handle that much velocity when she hits the table?"

Then Phil saw her spin end over end, hitting the springboard, next the table and then fly much higher and farther into the air than he'd ever dreamed might be possible, all while turning end over end. He thought
~~~

she might be twisting too, but it was hard to tell? *Were there special springs in the apparatus that let her do that?* he wondered.

The woman announcer, Eva Escanescue, gasped...

Phil watched Ell land, after all that incredible twisting and twirling, an astonishingly long distance from the table where she'd launched herself, right in the center of the lane. She was facing straight ahead, flexing her knees a little and then standing up and throwing her arms in the air! She made the landing look so effortless; you would have thought she'd just hopped down off a chair. She bowed toward the judges and then the other direction. Then Ell turned to trot back to a waiting area.

Phil turned to Joe Ingvul, one of his new friends on the USA Olympic wrestling team, who'd been watching as well. "Wow! I didn't know gymnasts could *do* that kind of stuff."

"Holy shit! They can't! *No one* can! That was out the *lock*!"

Venta, apparently having been stunned into silence, came back on the air, "I have... never... never seen a vault like that! I'm pretty sure that was a layout *double* with *two and a half twists* which has never been performed before in competition and I would have sworn... was impossible. Despite the fact that it must be the most difficult vault ever performed, I could *not* see anything about it that didn't show perfect, *absolutely perfect* form. Maybe the slow motion will show some errors, but the judges do their judging in real time. I can't imagine what they could *possibly* deduct for."

Escanescue stammered a little, "And, and, a double with even one twist has never been done before. Much less a double in the layout position! And, that had to be the biggest, highest, longest vault I've *ever* seen."

Phil's eyebrows rose as he noticed that the stands had erupted into pandemonium. Apparently a lot of other people thought that it was a pretty good vault too. Then the slow motion replay started showing. Phil's mouth fell open as he saw clearly for the first time just how much spinning and twisting had actually been going on during Ell's flight through the air! How could she possibly even land without hurting herself, much less land as elegantly as she had?

Radin Venta said, "Our analysis people tell me that the speed gun clocked her max speed during the sprint to the springboard to be just over 29 miles per hour! Michael Fentis has been the record holder for the fastest human, reaching 28.1 miles per hour at his fastest during the 100 meters! Of course she only runs about 25 meters for the vault, but Fentis doesn't reach top speed until about the 60th meter. This is so, so hard to believe! We'll have to have them clock it off the video to confirm. We're also trying to get confirmation that she just set world records for height and distance in addition to being the very first in the world to perform a vault that no one would have thought *could* be done! Even reviewing the slow motion video, I don't see *any* flaws in that vault. We may have just seen the best vault in *history*! The very best by a very, very large margin!"

Escanescue broke in, "The judges have actually given her a 10.0! That's not supposed to be possible anymore. No one has received or even gotten close to a 10 since they went back to the 10 point scoring system a few years back. But honestly, I don't know how they could have done otherwise. Half of the total of 10 points available are supposed to be for difficulty, and half for execution." She just did a vault of unheard of difficulty, which would immediately reset the bar for difficulty, and she did it *flawlessly*!

Venta said, "She's not going to take a second vault. She'd be absolutely crazy to try such a dangerous vault again after a *perfect* first try!"

Phil could hear the crowd going crazy in the background as the arena announcer boomed, "What a start to these Olympics! In one of the very first gymnastic events of the competition and in the very first Olympic event for this almost unknown gymnast she gets the first 10.0 score in decades!"

Ingvul punched Phil on the shoulder, "Man, your girlfriend is something else!"

Phil shook his head in bemusement, "She's *not* my girlfriend, but you don't know the *half* of her 'something else!'"

~~~

The big screens over the arena were showing Ell's vault over and over in slow motion while the crowd became increasingly giddy. Ell was called out for another bow. The team and coaches were beside themselves. She had not really expected her vault to cause *this* much commotion even if no one *had* ever done one like it before. She wondered whether or not to continue to do her best on the other events too. As Ell walked back from her second bow Anna stared at her wide eyed. Ell wondered what she might be thinking now. The stare morphed into a glare and, as Ell walked past, Anna hissed, "You have *got to be* taking drugs!"

Grinning foolishly Coach Benson came up and gave Ell a huge hug. She whispered in Ell's ear, "I'd say I knew
~~~

you could do it! But I had *no* clue. You're gonna ruin me as a coach if you tell the world I didn't think *anyone* could do a two and a half—two and a half! You know it'll be named a 'Donsaii' and no one else will *ever* be able to do one?" She stood back and clapped as Ell walked the rest of the way off the floor to her little corner.

On the net Venta said, "It's been brought to my attention that Donsaii has a history of performing at the highest levels only when it really matters. While other athletes crumble under pressure; those have been the times that she turns in her best performances. It's like she *thrives* on pressure! We can only wonder how this girl will perform in the other events under the crushing pressure of the Olympics? The vault's always been her best event, but will she deliver unbelievable, first ever performances in other events here at these Games?"

Ell looked up into the stands for her mother and grandmother. She picked them out because she knew their assigned seats. She shrugged her shoulders. Her mother shrugged hers back, then grinned and put both thumbs up and pumped her fist.

Ell decided that that meant her mom liked having her daughter kick some butt. *Should I keep going for it?* she wondered.

The bars were next and Coach tried to get Ell to warm up a little. This time she simply insisted on resting, trying to conserve everything she had for the actual performance. Benson looked at her for a moment as if she might try to *order* her to warm up. Then she grinned and shrugged her shoulders, "After *that* vault, I'd be *crazy* to try to tell you what to do." To the bewilderment of her teammates Ell lay down and actually took a brief nap while waiting for her turn to come up. Going into the zone always left her drained, so it was easy to drop off for a moment.

Benson shook her awake and Ell came up without any muzziness. As Ell walked out to the bars she was startled to hear a thunderous rush of applause. She looked around to see what'd happened but it wasn't obvious so she looked up at the big screens to see if they were replaying whatever'd occured. Her own face was in the monitors! The crowd was cheering before she even started! She felt her adrenalin levels start to spike and suppressed them with a couple of long calming breaths. As she stood and dusted her hands she looked around and to her astonishment realized that the girls at the other apparati were waiting to watch her on the bars too. She'd never seen anything like this at a meet before.

Apparently, they were all waiting to see if she produced another bit of Olympic gymnastic history and unwilling to miss it if she did. She shrugged, deciding that she would go ahead and do her very best on this routine too. She mentally reviewed her secret weapons for the bars.

After another deep breath she used her usual simple mount and then dropped into the zone, feeling the world slow. The arena became nearly silent as thousands of people held their breath. A couple swings around the upper bar, then she rocketed into the air above the bars for a double flip before catching the low; the first of the bar elements she had worked on after midnight when no one else was in the gym. When she finished the bars with a back triple dismount, she had performed three extremely high difficulty elements on the bars. Elements the world had never seen before. And she'd performed them like she owned them—

perfectly. As Ell stood from her flawless, wobble free stuck landing and threw her hands high, the arena exploded to its feet for another standing ovation. Ell looked around the arena as she came back down out of the zone and saw that gymnasts waiting at the other apparati had still not started their own routines. After a moment her eyes moistened as each and every one of the other gymnasts on the floor began applauding too! Shortly thereafter the judges awarded the second perfect 10 Olympic gymnastic score in decades and the big screens began showing her bar routine in slow motion. Over and over to admiring gasps.

Phil watched Ell's performance on the bars as soon as it came up on the net. Mesmerized by the dazzling perfection of her routine he almost didn't register Venta's words, "And I've just learned that this young woman, though a rising sophomore at the Air Force Academy, is only 16 years old! She's apparently so bright she skipped two grades and then left high school a year early! Not only a physical phenom, but an intellectual genius!"

Phil's heart sank as he realized that he'd tried to force himself on a fifteen or possibly, depending on her birth date, fourteen year old girl that Fall after their Physmed testing. The fact that he'd been unaware of her age, and at the time, not quite eighteen himself, didn't seem like an excuse.

And, she was his math tutor!

~~~

Ell finished the day with three 10s. There had been no doubt on beam where she again inserted two unimagined elements, but on the floor exercise the judges broke into vociferous arguments. Her floor
~~~

exercise also had three never before performed elements, just like the bars. No one could dispute the extreme, extreme difficulty of those elements nor the perfection of their execution. However, Ell'd never gone into her zone four times in the course of a single morning before and a floor exercise at about 90 seconds was pretty long for her. So, she not only performed a shorter exercise than most of the gymnasts, but placed most of the low energy dance and simpler acrobatic elements of the routine near the beginning. Half way through her planned routine she tried to go into the zone and failed, so she converted a planned triple into a double. She thought for a moment she might fall and the frightening possibility of the fall *did* drive her into the zone. Once in the zone she performed extraordinarily difficult elements back to back, including her three secret weapon elements that had never been performed by women... or men. One of the judges took exception to the easy-hard arrangement of the exercise and picked out some minor imperfections which, to everyone's surprise, fell in the easy first part of the exercise!

Nonetheless, Ell won four individual gold medals. As soon as she left the stand from receiving the last one for the floor exercise she was taken to an exam room where they took blood and urine specimens as well as performing a complete physical exam. Leaving the exam area she was mobbed by admirers and press. She signed hundreds of autographs, continuing long after Coach Benson tried to pull her away, trying to insist she rest.

The reporters were harder to handle. They put her at the front of the press room, sitting behind a table with a roomful of journalists peppering her with questions. "How do you feel after breaking more gymnastic records than anyone else in history?"

"Sir, I feel the same as I did early this morning." This got her a brief laugh.

"To what do you attribute these incredible feats?"

"Ma'am, I'm just lucky to have been born of very athletic parents and to be in a sport that matches my odd abilities."

"'Odd' abilities?!"

"Oh yes sir. I may be quick, but I have terrible endurance. I'm *very* lucky that gymnastics requires bursts of rapid maneuvering rather than staying power. I can hardly run a mile without throwing up."

"Really? Is that why you had a hard time with the longer floor exercise?"

"Yes Ma'am, I was tired from the other routines and worried that I couldn't stick it out for the whole routine. The two hundred meters seems like a pretty long race to me."

"That reminds me. Did you know that you clocked a higher speed than Michael Fentis' best in your sprint for the vault?"

Ell covered her mouth in dismay, "Oh *no*, that can't be!"

"Yes, yes, it's been checked, both the speed gun and the video frame count agree."

Ell blushed, her hand still on her mouth. She mumbled something that they couldn't pick up, but with enhancement later sounded like "Oops."

They continued to badger her with questions. She continued to speak with humility, be embarrassed by their admiration and to deflect as much glory as possible onto her teammates and their performances, which had also won some medals for Team USA. "You should be sure to interview Anna Kernova, our vault specialist, she got Bronze on the vault and you wouldn't believe that girl's tenacity and drive. And Kathy Voss got the Silver on beam with a great performance. If I hadn't gotten so lucky today she would have had the Gold. Irene Illman really put in a tremendous effort on floor, if she hadn't gone out of bounds she would have medaled too."

Rather than turning attention to the others as she had hoped, Ell's humility won her more admirers. Venta reported, "Ell Donsaii, appearing shy and not sure what to do with all the attention, claims she got lucky today, winning gold on all four apparati. However, luck didn't allow her to perform nine completely new elements of almost *unbelievable* difficulty, elements that almost everyone familiar with the sport would have predicted *were* impossible for ordinary humans. Ms. Donsaii is obviously not an ordinary human, and most of us who follow the sport would say she must be superhuman to have accomplished these feats. All drug testing has come back completely normal so far, but many of us will want to see if she can perform in the same fashion in the presence of Kryptonite won't we Eva?" he said, turning to Eva Escanescue.

Escanescue grinned, "Maybe we need to check her for Spidey bites?"

~~~

Phil won his match as expected and got on the bus back to their quarters. Since Ell had finished her part of the competition earlier in the day he was surprised to see her getting on the same bus as he was. She broke away from a huge crowd of reporters and trotted out. She looked like she was dragging a little getting on the
~~~

bus, but then she saw Phil and brightened up as she dropped into the seat next to him with her usual crooked little smile. “Phil! Hey, I saw you won your match. Sorry I didn’t get there in time to watch, but *way to go*!”

Phil stared at her, dumbfounded that Ell was congratulating him for his win. Taken aback actually, that she even knew how his match went. He, like everyone else at the Olympics and around the world, was stunned by what Ell Donsaii’d accomplished. Ell had gone from a little known dark horse to the most recognized athlete in the world over the course of a single day. Every sports and news outlet prominently featured video of her performances with flabbergasted announcers discussing at length just how impossible it was to do what she had just done. With a bemused expression he said, “Congratulations yourself. Not everyday that someone breaks every Olympic record in their sport in one day.”

Ell looked sheepish, “Yeah, I was a little out of control wasn’t I?”

“A little out of control, or way, way *in* control. One or the other.” Phil smiled at her.

~~~

The coaches isolated Ell from the press that night, insisting that the interviews they got right after the events would have to do. After warning her to get plenty of rest for the all-around tomorrow, they did sneak her mom and grandma in to see her that evening. Her mother threw her arms around her and whispered in her ear, “Ell! That was amazing! I knew you’d be able to do something special if you turned it loose, but WOW! I never thought it’d be something like that!”
~~~

Ell hugged her back fiercely. "Me either. I was pretty sure I'd win if I went for it, but I really didn't know that it would be by such a big margin." She leaned back and then drew her grandmother into a three way hug. "Maybe I shouldn't have thrown in so many of the new elements?"

"Yes you should have! If you're going to stop doing gymnastics anyway, you'd just as well do everything you can right now. Why not leave as big a mark as you can?"

"I guess you're right. I just worry that people are going to be too freaked out by the whole thing."

"You just go ahead and give it your all in the all-around tomorrow, freaked out people or not."

They spoke a while longer and then her mother and grandmother left so Ell could get her rest. Going deep into the zone four times that day had really taken it out of her and she actually slept six hours for the first time since the previous summer.

Chapter Seven

Hamid was in a frenzy. That morning they'd been set to board the first bus they saw with American Olympic athletes and take it hostage. Then an argument had broken out regarding how they would tell whether a bus had American athletes on board. While they were arguing, they looked up to see a bus passing that had several recognizable American athletes staring out the windows at them. Jamal had recognized Donsaii, his personal favorite, as one of them. That meant that the gymnastic team was likely on board. They had already decided that the high public recognition factor of the gymnasts made them the best targets, and they'd missed that target while arguing amongst themselves.

"Fools!" he shouted. "At *this* moment we would have been in the eye of the world if you'd followed orders instead of bickering!"

Jamal said, "Perhaps we should have..." but he was interrupted. Hamid told him to shut up and think for a moment.

After a pause Hamid asked for ideas.

Tentatively Jamal said, "Perhaps one of us should park where he can see the buses boarding. Then he can alert the rest of the team so it can stop and board that particular bus. A bus they'll *know* has the gymnastic team on it."

Hamid looked at Jamal suspiciously, "I suppose *you*

want to be the observer?"

"No, no, whoever you think is best."

Really, it was never in doubt, Jamal had the driver's license and was listed on the rental agreement. He knew his way around Dallas and he readily recognized the members of the gymnastics team. They bought radio based walkie talkies so Jamal would still be able to talk to the team after the team had started the portable net jamming device that they were taking onto the bus.

As the day's news came in, Hamid decided that Allah had stayed their hand that morning just so that Donsaii could have her day in the sun. Her instant and overwhelming fame on the net made her the *perfect* target for their plans. The eyes of the world would be much more focused as they killed her team members one by one, gradually leading up to the death of the world's most famous athlete!

Hamid's rage slowly diminished and he became ecstatic over the prospect!

Privately, Jamal wondered if Hamid's desire for killing, and the spotlight, was bigger than his desire for vengeance on America.

~~~

In the morning Jamal dropped the rest of the team off along the bus route just two and a half blocks from one of the normal boarding sites. Hamid led the team back into a small alley to await Jamal's notification. Jamal then drove to a vantage point where he could watch the buses board through binoculars. He sat in the SUV with a mixture of eager anticipation and dread. This gradually faded to boredom, but then his anxiety spiked as he saw some of the athletes filtering out to the bus stop. He didn't dare use the binoculars
~~~

constantly; someone might become curious. Hamid had decided to take whichever bus Donsaii boarded so Jamal simply watched for a feminine figure about 5' 9" tall with strawberry blond hair. He did have to use the binoculars once to check an individual of the right height who wore a stocking cap, but it wasn't her. The first and second buses left for the arena, then he saw Donsaii nimbly hop a small hedge and walk to the stop. He quickly checked with the binoculars, it was definitely her! "Aki," he said to his AI, "Get Hamid." When Hamid came on the line he said, "She's at the bus stop. I'll let you know when she boards."

Hamid simply said, "Okay."

A few moments passed, and he said, "Bus here, she's boarding. Bus is white with red and blue stripes. Number 3060, sign in front window says 'Olympic 16.'"

Again Hamid simply said, "Okay."

Once he'd identified the bus to the team, Jamal was to follow it in the Suburban and act as backup for any problems. After the bus pulled away from its stop he waited until it had gained two blocks on him. They all took the same route so he felt certain he wouldn't lose it.

He didn't want to draw any attention.

***

When the alarm went off, Ell still felt a little wrung out from the day before. Kathy, her roommate, bounced out of bed full of enthusiasm, so Ell let her have first crack at the bathroom. After a light breakfast they headed out to catch the bus to the arena. Surprised, Ell saw Phil near the back of the bus and headed back to sit with him. "Hey, I thought you'd be on a later bus. Isn't your first match around noon?"

"Yeah, but I wanted to watch the first part of the gymnastics all around before my match, I've got a friend in that competition."

Ell punched him lightly on the shoulder, "Yes you do! Isn't your coach gonna be pissed that you're watching an event instead of psyching yourself for your match?"

Phil shrugged, "Maybe," he winked at her, "but watching my friend is *important* to me. Besides *I* think I do best if I get my mind off a match for a while before the meet."

She grinned crookedly, "That's your excuse and you're stickin' to it?"

"Something like that."

"Good enough for me, I can use someone in my corner."

Phil grinned, "Ha, I think the whole world is in your corner."

A crooked grin again, "Really?"

"My God! Yes! Haven't you watched any of the news feeds? Everybody's crazy about you. I had to take a number with an exponent to be on your fan list, a big exponent!"

"Really? I haven't looked at any news feeds about gymnastics. Afraid I'll find out somebody disqualified me for something."

With astonishment Phil realized that she really hadn't checked the feeds. "Well, I'm sure they are gonna draw blood and take urine and hair samples to check for some banned substance in gallon lots that might explain how you just kicked gymnastic history on its ass. Maybe a whole body MRI scan?"

"Oh man! Again? They stuck me yesterday, I hate

that."

Ell's mildly petulant tone reminded Phil that she was much younger than everyone thought. "Hey," he said quietly, "what's this on the news about you being sixteen? Is that true?"

Ell clapped her hand over her mouth. She stared at him round eyed. "Oh no!" she mumbled. Her brows descended to express worry, "Did *that* come out on the news too? I've worked *so* hard to keep it a secret."

Phil gaped, "Why are you keeping it a secret? I'd think you'd be proud to have started college at fifteen?"

"No!" she said emphatically, shaking her head. "Everyone'll treat me like a *child*! Are they making a big deal about it on the net?" she asked, horrified. "Do you think *everyone's* going to know?"

Phil shook his head in amused exasperation at her naiveté, "*Everyone* will know. But don't worry; no one's going to treat someone with four gold medals like a little kid."

The bus had stopped at a corner. Phil and Ell, deep in conversation, didn't notice, though it was distinctly unusual. Even some argumentative voices near the front didn't distract them. Suddenly there was a loud bang and the sound of shattering glass. Ell and Phil looked up in startlement toward the front of the bus where they saw six swarthy men in US Olympic sweats pushing down the aisle.

Holding guns!

People were shouting and screaming.

Ell realized they wore store bought knock offs rather than regulation Team USA sweats. One of them shouted, "Shut up!" He pointed the gun at the roof of the bus and pulled the trigger. Another loud bang and silence descended on the bus. "You *are* our prisoners! We *will* kill each and every one who resists." He waved the gun slowly back and forth over the athletes as if daring anyone to say a word and be first to die.

Ell felt the zone crashing over her and she did nothing to stop it as she dropped her head behind the seat in front of her and whispered to her AI, "Allan, Call the police! This bus has been hijacked by terrorists!"

Allan said, "Sorry, something's blocking access to the net. I can't even get through using military push. I suspect they're carrying a jammer."

Ell's world had slowed. In a whispered tone, "Phil, they're blocking the net!" She looked up and saw Beretta written on the gun in the hand of the nearest terrorist.

"Crap!" he said, low out of the corner of his mouth, eyes focused on the gun.

"Somebody's got to get out and call the cops! Can you bust out through a window?"

"I can bust a window, but I'm too big to get through the frame in a hurry. I'll break, you jump." With that, Phil stood, put his carry bag in front of the glass, and drove a back elbow into the bag. He looked on in startlement when the entire window popped out into the street.

To Phil and the terrorist next to him, Ell seemed to explode headfirst out through the window. She was in the bus one moment and *gone* out the window in the next.

For Ell, deep in her zone, it seemed to take forever for the glass to move out of her way and for her to launch herself out the opening. She carefully applied spin so that she tumbled end over once, landing on her feet. She placed those feet meticulously to land beside, and not on the window which was still skidding over the pavement as cracks crazed their way across the safety glass. Then she leaned to her right and accelerated back down the street in the direction the bus had come from, saying, “Allan, let me know when you have contact with the net again! Report to the police.” She felt like she was moving in slow motion despite her efforts to cover ground as rapidly as possible. At the sound of gunshots behind her, she began jinking side to side. A few bullets struck in her vicinity, though none were at all close. She glanced back in hopes that someone else had made it out the window and in dread that they might have been hit by the bullets. No one else was on the street besides Ell and three non Olympic pedestrians who were actively diving for cover.

In awe, Phil watched Ell’s agile landing followed by an incredible burst of speed. She ran back in the direction the bus came from. Suddenly he realized that the terrorist, who had leaned over him to look out the window Ell had just jumped through, had now thrust an arm out the window and begun shooting wildly in Ell’s direction. Phil cast an arm up, across the terrorist’s chest and over his shoulder. Phil then ripped the terrorist out of the window frame, grabbing the wrist with the pistol as it came back into the bus and tumbling them both to the floorboards. Moments later two other pistols were pointed at his head. He slowly let go of the terrorist he’d pulled out of the window, raising his hands. The man he’d pulled out of the window scrambled to his feet and began kicking Phil in the ribs while screaming in Arabic. Phil simply tensed his highly developed musculature. The kicks bounced off relatively harmlessly.

A terrorist with a deformed nose shouted and the kicking stopped. Then in English he screamed at Phil, "Get up! Was that *Donsaii* who escaped?!"

Phil shrugged and started to rise to his seat. This effort was handily stopped by the insertion of the business end of a pistol into his eye socket. "I *said*, 'Was that Donsaii that escaped?'"

Phil looked into the fierce eyes behind the crooked nose and shrugged again, "Yep."

More shouting in Arabic ensued, but Phil was allowed to slowly get back into his seat.

~~~

About a hundred meters behind the bus Allan spoke in Ell's ear, saying "I've now reached the net and reported the hijacking of the bus."

Ell said, "Call me a taxi!" Then she saw a large black SUV coming down the street toward her. She stepped out into the street, waving for it to stop. It pulled over and she opened the passenger door, consciously slowing her speech to say, "That bus up there's been hijacked by terrorists! It's full of Olympic athletes. *Follow* it so we can report its location to the police." Ell swung into the passenger seat, assuming the driver would comply with her instructions. The driver's swarthy Arabic appearance registered only as she saw his right hand swing toward her carrying another 9mm Beretta! She grasped the barrel before he could point it at her and twisted it to her right, his left. Just like her self defense course had taught, that direction loosened his fingers and the gun didn't fire. She continued rotating it until it pointed back at him, mildly surprised
~~~

that it didn't fire through the entire evolution.

~~~

Jamal'd been following about two blocks behind the bus. He'd been wondering whether this was his opportunity to pull himself out of this mess. He could be just a little late when they went into the parking deck for their suicidal mission. Then, if he didn't go in himself, they'd be unable to come back out after him in pursuit. Perhaps he could find a way to lose himself in America and develop a new identity? As he followed the bus he was surprised to see something fall out of the side of the vehicle, two things actually. *Ah, one was a window*; the other was a person who landed on his feet without even stumbling, despite the fact that the bus must have been traveling 20 miles an hour! The man started running down the street toward Jamal. Fast!

The walkie talkie buzzed and Hamid said roughly in Arabic, "Donsaii's escaped! Catch or kill her!"

Jamal's eyes widened as he realized that the person running toward him was actually the young girl gymnast. He recognized her reddish blond hair now. He could hardly believe her speed as she ran toward him and thought to himself that there wouldn't be any way he could catch her. Then he realized, with some bemusement, that he didn't want to catch her. Just watching her on TV, Jamal'd begun to admire her. He'd been entranced by her looks even before she broke so many gymnastic records the day before. He found her humbleness when she'd been interviewed inspiring. Now she streaked down the street toward him. He slowed the SUV while considering the absurdity of the notion that it could even be possible for him to
~~~

apprehend someone *that* fast.

Then, to Jamal's amazement, Donsaii slowed and stepped out in front of his vehicle, waving her arms at him, obviously wanting *him* to stop for her! For a moment he considered warning her off. Surely it would be okay to spare this young girl he so admired? It'd be hard to explain to Hamid though. Hamid would certainly be watching from the back of the bus.

Jamal decided to capture her and then find a way to avoid joining the others in the parking deck. He stopped and she pulled open the passenger door, getting in without being asked and rapidly saying something about following the bus! To be sure he had control of the situation Jamal lifted his Beretta out of the cup holder and turned it toward her. To his astonishment, before he had fully pointed it at her, she snatched the pistol out of his hand and pointed it back at him. It happened so quickly and *so violently* that at first he thought she'd simply hit him on the back of his hand.

She said, "Catch, up, to, the, bus." Her tone was matter of fact, not demanding, simply telling him what to do. Her words were jerky as if she was trying hard to enunciate clearly.

He stared into the muzzle of his own gun for a moment, then shrugged and pulled the SUV back out into the road to follow the bus.

"Faster," she said, and he complied.

When they'd pulled within 20 meters of the bus, she rolled down the passenger window and, with an impossibly quick movement, pushed her shoulders up and out, pointing the Beretta. Then, without firing a shot, she dropped back down into the seat. "It's still on safe!" she said with a hint of amusement as she looked the gun over for the safety. Jamal felt his face flush with embarrassment. Then she was back up out the window. She fired a burst like a machine gun! Jamal hadn't even been aware that the gun *had* an automatic fire mode. He thought to himself that she was a terrible shot. She didn't break a single window at the back of the bus. He could see Hamid's crooked nose in the back window of the bus, a startled look on his face.

"Drop back!" She said to him.

"Huh?" Jamal said, suddenly noticing that the bus was listing to the right. A large strip of rubber flew off of the right rear tire and the bus swayed drunkenly. Jamal saw Hamid kicking at one of the back windows and he hit the brakes.

"Drop back a hundred meters so we can get back on the net!" She demanded.

The bus swayed the other way as large fragments of rubber came off of the left rear tires as well.

Hamid succeeded in kicking out a back window and began shooting at them! As near as Jamal could tell, none of his shots even struck the SUV, but Jamal braked to a complete stop just as the bus turned into the parking deck with sparks flying off the rear wheel rims. She said, "Follow them."

Jamal said, "That's as far as they're going."

"What?"

"They've got a hiding place in that parking deck."

"What? Why? They can't hope to escape once they're holed up in there!"

"They don't plan to escape. It's a suicide mission."

She blinked at him in dismay, "They're going to *kill* them?"

Jamal nodded. "They'll kill all the athletes, and then themselves in a blaze of glory. First though, they will negotiate deals, preach their philosophy on the net news and otherwise drag out the agony."

Her eyes glanced up at her HUD and she said, "Allan, are you getting this out to the police?"

Jamal realized that she was speaking to her AI. His walkie talkie barked Arabic at him in Hamid's voice. "Jamal! What are you doing? Get that bitch in control and bring her down here."

Jamal picked up the radio, "Sorry, she took my gun. That's what she's been shooting at you with."

"Fool!" After a pause, "The wild way she was shooting she can't have any bullets left. I can't believe she lucked out and hit our tires. Grab her and drag her down here. She's *just* a girl!"

Jamal's scalp prickled as he suddenly realized that blowing out all four of the tires in the back of that big bus didn't happen by accident. Those tires were big and tough. She'd been intentionally shooting at the tires! *That* was why she hadn't hit any windows. In English he said to her, "How many rounds did you fire?"

Distractedly she replied, "Three for each tire, so twelve, plus one that missed high and right. How many in the mag?"

More hair standing up. She knew exactly how many shots she'd taken and exactly how many hit their targets! How? She'd been firing on automatic hadn't she? "Uh, Fifteen, plus one in the chamber."

"So, I still have three bullets, don't get any ideas." She looked down from her HUD and over at him. "Are you with them or against them? You need to decide ASAP!"

It startled Jamal to realize that she recognized how conflicted he was. "I used to be one of them. I've wanted to get out for some time, but if I try to leave they'll kill me."

"Well, maybe if you help, you can get into witness protection or something. But you need to help big. Where's their hideout?"

Jamal paused, heard sirens in the distance, then decided she was his best chance. "In the back corner of the bottom level."

"Okay, get out. We'll wait for the cops."

~~~

Jamal hopped out. Ell opened her door at the same time and then stood on the inside of the door so that her head and shoulders stuck up out of the vehicle. Holding the Beretta in plain view she said, "Walk around to this side." He did so and then she got the rest of the way out and closed the door. Moments later three police cars pulled up, lights flashing. They screeched to a halt next to Ell and Jamal. Doors burst open and police stepped out behind them, weapons drawn. One of them spoke over a megaphone, "Drop that weapon! Now!"

Ell flicked on the safety and tossed the Berretta into the grass, putting up her hands and allowing herself to drop out of the zone. A moment later she and Jamal were surrounded by police with drawn weapons. One said, "Wait a minute, this is the Donsaii kid!"

"Who?!"

"The girl that broke all the records in gymnastics yesterday!"

They all stared at her a moment then several voices at once said, "Naw," and "She's just a look alike?" and "Why would she be out here?" and "She's just a kid!"

The first cop said, "No, that's her all right. My daughter made me watch her over and over last night!" He turned to Ell, "What are you doing in this
~~~

neighborhood?" He frowned, "And carrying a weapon?"

Ell stared at him and said in a measured tone, "As I reported over the net, the Team USA bus to the sports arena was hijacked. I escaped. The bus has just been driven down to the lowest level of the parking deck behind me."

The cops stared at her incredulously, then wildly about the area, exclaiming. Some seemed to believe her, but others looked doubtful in the extreme.

Sounding calm, Ell said, "May I give you a feed of the hijacking from my AI?"

More sirens were sounding in the distance as the first policeman nodded. Ell had Allan feed him the video recording from the time of the bus boarding, right up to her escape out the window. She suppressed the feed of her stopping Jamal and especially of her shooting at the bus.

Exclamations followed from the surrounding police then several of them got back into their vehicles and began slowly following the bus down into the lower levels of the parking deck. Jamal was handcuffed and he and Ell taken aside for questioning.

More and more police arrived and a mobile command post pulled up with senior officers to direct the response.

Second responders cordoned off the area.

A SWAT team arrived and began poring over structural drawings of the deck they downloaded from the net.

Ell told her story over and over and repeatedly introduced Jamal as a former member of the terrorist team, now seeking asylum and witness protection. The rapid accumulation of huge numbers of law enforcement personnel astonished Ell, who had no idea the extent of the preparations that had been made for the possibility of terrorists at the Olympics. She kept expecting them to *do* something to rescue her friends and became more and more frustrated when no visible progress occurred.

She was answering the same question about how she'd come into contact with Jamal for the *ninth* time when Allan said, "Ell, the terrorists are broadcasting now."

Ell immediately broke off her conversation and looked up at her HUD. She saw the Arab with the crooked nose who she'd seen shooting at her from the back of the bus. He stood in front of the camera with an excited and agitated look on his face. He'd removed his Olympic gear and donned a checked keffiyeh and a black garment that looked like a floor length shirt. In the background of the frame, Team USA athletes sat on the floor with their knees drawn up. Their AI headbands had been removed. After a moment Ell realized that their wrists were handcuffed beneath their knees in that position. While watching she sank to the floor and put her hands in the same position. It wasn't difficult to bring her hands out from behind her knees to her front while clasped to one another as if handcuffed, but it would certainly take precious moments if you were trying to do it quickly. Ell suspected that those who were less flexible might find it impossible. No doubt it would quickly become uncomfortable. Ell picked out Phil and her teammates, noting with relief that they all seemed uninjured though she could see some of the girls sobbing. Phil looked angry.

The man with the deformed nose looked off screen a moment, then squinted at the camera. Apparently realizing that it was on, he cleared his throat, "Allah

Akbar! I am Hamid Asghar and my name is a name that you *will* remember and remember for a *very* long time." His thick accent made his English difficult, but not impossible to understand. "In response to the treachery of Christians over the centuries, and in accordance with our war against the Great Satan America, we have captured these Olympic athletes and will kill them, one by one, until our demands are met!" He held up a finger, "Our first demand, return Ell Donsaii to us! You have one hour!"

Because of the man's accent, at first Ell didn't parse what the demand had been, then ice washed over her. She fought to keep from going into the zone from her intense emotional reaction. The detective who'd been questioning her thought her deep breathing was a panicked reaction to the possibility that they might actually turn her over to the terrorists and said, "Hey, hey. Don't worry. There's no way anyone's going to turn you over to those animals."

He was startled by the fierceness of her gaze when she turned back to him. "No, that's *exactly* what you need to do. Turn me over to them. Now!"

The detective leaned back in his chair with raised eyebrows. "We are *not* going to turn the star of the Olympics over to terrorists!"

"Broker a deal. Get them to let ten of the athletes go in order to have me. Ten lives for one would be a good deal." Ell's voice was uninflected, but she rocked him further back in his chair with the intensity of her gaze.

"No! We're done here. We're sending you back to the stadium to compete."

"I, am, not, going!"

~~~
~~~

Ell found herself being bundled into the back of a police car, in the protective custody of two cops who'd been detailed to deliver her back to the gymnastics arena. The policemen had not, however, been told to keep her prisoner, so at the next light she simply opened the door and got out, turning to trot back toward the parking deck. The cop in the passenger seat leapt out to come after her while the other one turned the car around. When the cop caught up to her he said, "Now look here young lady!" and reached for her arm.

She turned, deftly avoiding his hand, crossed her arms, stood with a wide based stance and stared at him with her intense, intimidating green eyes. "What?! Am I under arrest? If so, please make my crime known to me!"

"Uh..."

"I thought not." She turned and continued down the street. When she arrived, she strode directly to the command post truck, easily dodged the hand of the cop detailed to keep civilians out and opened the door, stepping into the air conditioned interior, then closing and locking the door behind her. Immediately the guard cop outside began twisting the knob, then knocking, first gently then more forcefully.

In order to determine who was in charge, Ell rapidly took in the dynamics of the people inside the truck. Feeling the lines of power radiating from a grizzly, gray haired man in the back of the room, she watched him intently for a moment. He intermittently listened to others and barked orders at the people staring at the multiple screens in the front. One of the men was reporting to him, "Chief, there's no way we're going to break into their hideout without casualties. It's a damned fort! Eighteen inch concrete walls. Heavy gauge steel doors. If we used explosives strong enough to break in quickly, we'd kill or injure a lot of the hostages. Other entry methods will be so slow that the terrorists will be able kill most of the athletes with those assault weapons we saw in the broadcast."

Ell strode his way.

The chief looked up at her, "Who is *that*?!"

The man with his back to her turned in curiosity, then jerked around. It was the detective who'd had her bundled off!

Ell strode up to the Chief, read his nametag and put out her hand, "Chief Bowers, I'm Ell Donsaii, the person that the terrorists are demanding. Please trade me for as big a group of the other athletes as you can."

The chief barked a laugh and the detective reached out to grab Ell's arm. She simply moved out of his reach. The chief said, "We don't trade hostages! *Certainly* not an underage girl."

"Trade me for ten hostages. The ethics of the situation are inescapable—one life for ten." Ell deftly sidestepped another grab by the detective.

"Listen young lady," the detective began, pulling out his handcuffs and shaking them loose, then reaching out again for her wrist. "*You're* gonna be in protective custody! I don't care how famous you are..."

Ell's hands moved violently and he stumbled to a stop, staring at his wrists which were suddenly manacled with his own handcuffs.

Ell continued to stare at the chief, "As you can see, I'm more capable than one might assume. *If* you would simply turn me over to them, I believe that I will be able to disarm many of the terrorists and in other ways impede their efforts."

For a moment the chief stared, startled, at the

detective's bound wrists, then looked at Ell in musing appraisal. After a moment, he shook his head and said, "Sorry no." In a louder voice he said, "Arrest this young lady and put her in protective custody." To his astonishment, before he finished the sentence she'd covered the three steps to the door, jerked it open, pulling it open so violently that the guard cop who'd been outside pushing on it fell into the room. She slipped past the guard to the outside. By the time they reached the door and looked out, she was trotting down the street away from the cordoned off crime scene area.

"Shall we pursue?" one of the street cops asked.

The chief looked after her for a moment, then shrugged and waved dismissal. "Nah, we got bigger fish to fry. *And* it would be a media nightmare..."

~~~

Ell stalked down the street, tears in her eyes. She couldn't for the life of her figure out why she was crying? She'd only known her gymnastics team mates a few months and *none* of them had even been nice to her. That big lunk, Phil, had certainly never given her much reason to like him, though she had to admit he'd been friendlier recently. Still, her mind's eye kept calling up her last view of him on her HUD, on his knees with his wrists cuffed beneath his thighs. The people around him were just blurs, but Phil's face was clear to her, a mixture of belligerence and apprehension on it.

She felt sure that if she could get into that room, in the zone, she could do *something* to help. Why *had* she jumped out of the bus? At the time it'd seemed logical, but now it seemed the rankest cowardice to have left Phil and the others' behind and fled to safety herself.
~~~

There didn't seem to be any way that she could possibly get back in there. If only she'd stayed, she might've been able to go into the zone and use her quickness to do something to save the others.

Then she realized she was passing a uniform store. She slipped in. Did they have police uniforms? Yes! She found pants and a blouse in her size and put them on over her gymnastic leotard. Then she found a salesperson who introduced herself as "Mabel, the owner." Mabel commented that Ell looked familiar, but didn't make the connection without Ell's Olympic gear. She found Ell a blank name tag, black socks, a belt, cap and regulation shoes. Ell put on the entire uniform and they inspected her image in the mirror. Ell was astonished at the change in her own appearance. "Alrighty Miss, you look very official. How many sets would you like to order?"

Ell realized that the store would normally be outfitting new police who needed several uniforms at least. "Uh, just this one until I get it approved by the sergeant."

"Really? Okay. I'll need to see your police ID to be able to approve the sale. Don't want folks impersonating officers you know."

Ell looked at her like a deer in the headlights for a moment.

Mabel just had time to realize that impersonating an officer was exactly what the girl had in mind before said girl bolted out the door in the uniform. She was much too quick for Mabel to apprehend. Mabel wondered to herself, *What could that kid be thinking? We had her on the security cameras, my AI captured images, and her bare hands had to have left DNA all over stuff here.* She shrugged and asked her AI to file a report with the police. She knew it'd be a while before they responded, what with the terrorists holed up down the street... Mabel's eyes widened.

Thinking of the terrorists and their attack on the Olympians a few blocks away caused her to realize why the girl looked familiar. That was Ell Donsaii! She pondered having her AI call the thief in as being Donsaii in order to get the incident higher priority than shoplifting usually got, then shook her head. Mabel had marveled while watching the young woman's accomplishments and felt a great deal of pride that Ell represented Mabel's country. For all she knew, the girl might be responding to the terrorists' attack on her fellow Olympians and *needing* to impersonate a police officer for some reason. Mabel decided that if *Ell Donsaii* wanted to steal something from Mabel's store, Ell Donsaii could have it. She told her AI to retract the police report.

~~~

Hamid came back on the net and announced that the Americans had 15 minutes to deliver Donsaii or one of the athletes would die. "Allah Akbar!"

~~~

Ell straightened her uniform and walked quickly back to the parking deck, wondering just how she was going to make the rookie cop uniform work to get her into the terrorists' hideout. It was getting hot as the sun got higher in the sky on a Texas morning and sweat prickled on her. As she walked up to the area of the command center a cop stepped out of one of the big support vehicles with Jamal, who had his wrists cuffed in front of him. The cop with Jamal was looking around as if searching for someone, "You there," he motioned with his chin to Ell, "can you take this guy downtown and book him into protective custody?"

Ell realized that the policeman had just been looking for someone lower in the pecking order than himself. Ell's rookie appearance had made her an obvious choice. "Yes sir." She said to the officer. Hoping desperately that she wasn't making some procedural error, she walked up to Jamal and grasped him by the arm, "Come along now."

Jamal's eyes widened as he recognized Ell, but he said nothing as she led him down a side street. Without looking at him she said, "I need to get down into the terrorists hideaway, do you know of a way I can get in?"

Jamal looked at her doubtfully, "They'll *kill* you."

She nodded, "They'll try. Can you get me in?"

"You wouldn't be able to take any weapons with you, you'll be thoroughly searched."

"That's okay, can you get me in?"

"Can you cut me loose?"

She turned into an alley that Jamal immediately recognized. It was the one that had the entrance to the storm drain! Ell led Jamal behind a dumpster where she inspected the cheap plasticuffs on his wrists. They were made out of the same material as standard cable ties. "Wait here." She turned and strode away. Jamal pondered fleeing, but he would surely be re-apprehended, running down the street alone with his wrists cuffed. He sank to the ground in the slightly cooler shade behind the dumpster and wondered if he could play both sides of this match? He asked his AI to contact Hamid. He'd been astonished when the police left his AI on his belt and HUD on his head. He'd assumed they'd disabled it. To his surprise, his AI responded, “Working.”

Jamal was even more surprised a few seconds later when Hamid came on. “Jamal, you coward, what are you doing?”

“The American police captured me, but I escaped. Now I’ve captured Donsaii and I’m bringing her to the secret entrance for you.”

“What?! I don’t believe you! Let me see her!”

Oops. Jamal thought desperately, then, “I’ve stashed her for the moment. I’ll show her to you when I pick her up to bring her down.”

“You *will* come to the secret entrance, with or without her. If the Americans follow you, I’ll personally kill you before they harm any of us.”

~~~

Back in the command post one of the techs at the front of the truck spun and shouted, “Chief Bowers! We’ve extracted communication to and from Hamid off the net. It’s that Jamal, saying that he’s captured Donsaii and is bringing her to their hideout!” The tech tapped his HUD meaningfully.

The Chief cursed and looked up at his own screens as the feed came in but it was just audio. When he’d heard the conversation he swore some more. “Who let that Jamal guy go! Jeffers! Track that down for me! Jones! I thought you said there wasn’t any way into the bottom of that deck without blowing a hole?!”

“Jeez Chief, the *plans* sure as hell don’t show any ingress! Maybe they dug a tunnel when they were setting this up? Sure as hell they’ve been planning this for a while to have strung the antenna they’re accessing the net through.”

Bowers fixed Jones with a fierce glare, “Figure it
~~~

out," he grated, "We *need* that back door for ourselves and we sure as Hades have got to keep them from getting Donsaii *in* through it. There'll be Hell to pay if they kill *that* girl! *And* get me better audio of what's happening inside the terrorist hideout!"

"Sorry Chief. They've caulked under the door so we can't slip in a mike or camera. We're having to use a laser mike on the door and the door's too big and heavy to transmit audio very well."

Chief Bowers turned again, "White, what's SWAT up to? You figured out a way to get in yet?"

White looked up from his station, "No sir. Sorry. Those steel doors've been welded shut. We've set shaped charges to blow in the small door or cut a hole in one of the concrete walls, but without knowing where the athletes are located in that room it's highly likely that the explosion would hurt or kill one or more of our own people. We can use a cutter to get through the door, but it'd take forever."

"Can't you drive your assault truck through that big door?"

"No sir. Analysis of the video they broadcast shows they've parked the bus behind that door."

"Don't you have some kind of ram you can mount on the front of the truck to push in the smaller door?"

"It's a very solid door and opens outward, we might only bend it in and then the truck might get stuck. We have a lance for the truck that would punch a hole through the door, then it has a hook so that we can back up and pull the door out of its frame, but it'd take time and those Kalashnikovs they're carrying could kill a *lot* of hostages before we got anyone in the door."

The chief put his hands to his head and looked up at the ceiling. "Jesus Christ!" he muttered, then louder to the room in general, "*Anybody* gets any great ideas, let me know pronto." He turned to his second in command, "Do you think he'll really kill one of them?"

His second turned palms up and shrugged.

~~~

Ell stepped around the corner of the dumpster with a new pair of wire cutters from an Ace Hardware on the next block. As she cut Jamal's wrists loose she also asked, "Will he really kill one of them?"

Jamal shrugged, "Without a doubt. If I'm to take you to them, you'll have to act like you're my captive. Take off the hat and jacket and I will send Hamid video showing you as my captive so that they'll let us in."

Ell looked at him warily a moment, then shrugged out of the jacket, hung it and the cap on the dumpster and turned her back to the wall. Jamal handed her the plastic strap handcuffs she'd just cut off of him. "Put these on and kneel so that it looks like I have you in control." Ell put them around her wrists with the breaks on the back side where they wouldn't be visible. Jamal framed her in his HUD so that just her upper body in the light blue police shirt was visible. By itself the shirt didn't look much like a uniform. "Look intimidated." he said and Ell turned her eyes down at the ground. He contacted Hamid. "Here she is."

"Hah! You really have her! Okay bring her in, but remember what I said about being followed."

~~~

The Chief's eyes widened as the tech directed Hamid's feed to him. He bellowed, "Get that image out over the net to all personnel in the area. Reddish blond hair, light blue shirt, with an Arabic man. They *must* be nearby. They'd *better* not get down into that deck or we'll *all* be in deep, deep, *deep* shit! All eyes on deck!"

~~~

To Ell's surprise, Jamal stepped out from behind the dumpster, walked about fifty feet further down the alley and then bent over a manhole cover.

He stuck a finger into the hole on one side and tried to lift it. It didn't budge. Jamal swore. "It's stuck!"

Ell said, "Let's find another one."

"No! This is the one that leads to the redoubt."

"What do you mean? They've got to interconnect!"

"Maybe. But *this* is the one *I* know how to find the redoubt from."

She knelt, pulled out her wire cutter, pulled opened the handles and stuck one in the pick hole at the side of the manhole cover. Then she grabbed the handle that stuck up and said, "Help me pull." They heaved together and the cover came up. They quickly climbed the rungs down into the cooler interior. Jamal reached up to try to pull the cover back over the hole.

Just then Allan called Ell's attention to her HUD where she saw Hamid angrily denouncing America while two of his compatriots dragged one of the Olympians up to a wall. Hamid said, "You've failed to deliver on our first demand. Donsaii hasn't been brought to us. We're going to demonstrate just how serious we are!" With that, he wheeled away from the camera and his Berretta came into view pointing at the athlete. It was one of the girls! The girl struggled, violently jerking from side to side so Ell couldn't be sure, but she thought it was her nemesis Anna Kernova, the vaulter!

Ell shouted at Jamal, "Leave it, let's go!" As she
~~~

climbed down the rungs Ell fought to stay out of the zone, though the scene on her HUD horrified her. She saw the two men pull the girl's arms apart as she shrieked and struggled fiercely between them. Hamid's Berretta fired as the girl twisted in their grip.

The girl shrieked even louder and Hamid turned back to the camera. Excitement gleamed in his eyes. "So," he said, "she moved and the bullet didn't kill her outright."

The camera moved closer and Ell could see that it was definitely Anna, holding her left side and sobbing on the floor.

Hamid said, "You see now what happens when you defy me! In my mercy I won't shoot her again. Yet! I'll leave her fate in *your* hands and the hands of Allah! Do as I say and we'll let her go if she's still alive! You have one hour to meet our next demand or we will shoot another athlete. The next one, I *will* shoot until dead. To comply, you must close down the Olympics. Empty the arenas and announce to the world that you've abandoned these crass commercial endeavors! Don't forget I'm also still waiting for you to deliver Donsaii."

~~~

Chief Bowers barked, "Start that sixty minute timer over. White! Analyze that video to figure out where to blow your way in with the lowest friendly casualties possible, SWAT goes in *before* the hour's up! Jones, have you figured out their back door yet?"

Jones looked up, "No sir! We searched on foot, but haven't found any evidence of recent digging around the deck. Maybe they dug their way in through the storm drainage system, we're going to send folks down into it."

"GO, GO, GO!"
~~~

White said, "There's no way we can blow a hole in a foot and a half thick concrete without producing shrapnel that hurts people inside Chief! Permission to start cutting into the wall to weaken it?"

"Yes, yes! But I'll bet they hear you and threaten to kill someone if you don't stop, so figure you're going to have to blow your way in anyway."

The Chief kept barking orders, "Smitty! Find some video of everyone leaving the stadium yesterday and see if you can dress it up and revise the timestamp so it looks like everyone's leaving today. Cut the terrorists' antenna and insert yourself so we can approve any contact he gets from the outside. Do it so you can insert that video of folks leaving and try to make it look like it's a news-feed. Get the mayor to provide a video statement for us to feed them, one saying he's canceling the Olympics."

~~~

Jamal only led Ell a few feet through the storm drains before it became too dark to see. Neither of them had a flashlight and he thought they'd have to go back. To his surprise she stepped in front, took his hand and began leading confidently down the tunnel. "I've got a military AI with infrared lights and receivers. I can lead, but how will we know that we've arrived at their hideout?"

Jamal said, "There are two manholes then the next one's the entrance. It's an overhead grate rather than a manhole tube like what we came down."

She continued leading him silently. He could tell when they passed each of the two manhole tubes by the sound of traffic overhead and one of the manhole covers leaked a little light. Then Ell whispered, "I see a
~~~

big grate just ahead, I want to go see what I can see. Stay here a moment."

Jamal could see light spilling down through the drain grate from the hideout. The grate was propped up on one edge. Hamid had ordered it left in this position, propped open with a two by four so that they could exit quickly if needed. Ell walked closer to the opening, then turned to the side of the tunnel where rungs were welded and stepped up until her head was just below the entrance. Jamal saw her detach and unwind something from the front of her HUD headband and slowly raise it with one hand. He remembered that someone was supposed to be guarding the opening! He moved closer so that when the guard saw her he could claim to have brought her.

~~~

Ell carefully studied her HUD as it showed her the intake from the tiny detachable camera she'd lifted off her headband. The bus was on the far side of the room with a huge, metal, garage door behind it. Several large cardboard boxes and a welder were near the front of the bus. A portapotty stood next to it. One of the Arabs stood by an ordinary metal door in the far corner with an assault rifle. Another leaned against the wall about ten feet from the storm drain. The rest of them seemed to be arguing amongst themselves near the bus. She counted seven of the terrorists, though she couldn't be sure there weren't some in the bus. The athletes still sat in their handcuffs in the middle of the room except for three that clustered near one wall.

Ell recognized two of the girls from the gymnastic team huddled over another who was lying down, presumably Anna. She looked back at the big group and
~~~

saw Phil's broad shoulders. The man who presumably was supposed to be guarding the storm drain lit a cigarette. Ell considered trying to attack him and take his assault weapon, but she didn't recognize the weapon type and might not be able to find the safety or use it well. If he carried a Berretta like Jamal's, she couldn't see it. Her use of the weapon to shoot at the bus tires gave her confidence in a Beretta. Not only did she know the location of the safety, but she also had intimate knowledge of its kick because the kick lifting the muzzle had made her miss her second shot at a tire on the bus. She decided she had to get out in the midst of them in order to get one of their Berettas, assuming someone besides Jamal was carrying one.

Ell descended the rungs to go get Jamal and then realized he'd already come up behind her. She whispered to him, "Ok, take me in and turn me over to them."

Jamal whispered back. "I'm not going in there! I'll call out that I've delivered you and that I'm going back out into the city. You're *crazy* to go in there!"

She shrugged, "Ok, call out."

He looked at her a moment more, whispered, "Crazy." Then he tipped his head back and called out, "Hamid, I've brought Donsaii."

A moment later the guard loomed over the drain opening and pointed his rifle down at them. "Send her up," he barked in Arabic. Ell's AI translated it for her just before Jamal repeated it in English as well.

Ell started back up the rungs. She had no difficulty acting fearful. She recognized that this was certainly the most dangerous thing she'd ever done. She ruthlessly suppressed the zone, not wanting to go into it now and then find herself exhausted when she actually needed to be in it. She hesitated near the top.

Hamid appeared and said, "Get up here! Jamal, don't you move!" He pointed a Beretta, presumably at Jamal.

Ell slowly climbed two more rungs. She said, "You'll let some of the others go right?"

Hamid laughed, "I'm not trading anyone for you." Impatiently, he knelt and grabbed for her. Ell had to restrain the impulse to avoid his grab, but when he ripped upward on the cloth at her shoulder she just let the loose shirt slip up over her head. Surprised at the lack of resistance he fell back onto his buttocks. Embarrassed, he lunged forward again and grabbed the shoulder strap on her leotard. Worried that he would rip the strap, Ell came up with him when he pulled this time. The lack of resistance overbalanced him and he fell back again, pulling Ell over on top of him. She considered trying to take his Beretta, but she was a long away from the rest of the terrorists. Instead she scrambled off him, then crouched on her knees, trying to look non-threatening. Hamid rose to his feet, stood over her a moment, then clubbed her to the ground. Ell saw the blow coming and rolled with it, but it still hurt. She lay as if dazed and passively allowed Hamid and another guard to drag her by the feet over to the middle of the room with the other athletes. Through slitted eyes she saw the two men's eyes fixed on her body as it bumped along behind them. Ell's AI translated for her as they started arguing about whether to broadcast her capture on the net. Hamid wanted to broadcast it as a triumph, but the other, named Arat, pointed out that it would alert the Americans to the presence of a back entrance. When they dropped her near the other athletes she looked around, trying to appear dazed. Arat knelt to cuff her wrists while Hamid went back to yell at Jamal. Arat rolled her over to her stomach, managing to fondle her breast while doing so, then pulled her wrists back and cuffed them to one another and left her on her stomach. He pulled off her AI and tossed it and the HUD headband across the room to where the other athletes' AIs lay in a messy pile.

Face against the floor, but turned towards the others. Ell saw Phil scooting on his butt over to her location. He leaned over her and whispered, "Ell! Are you okay?"

The concern in Phil's voice gave Ell a warm feeling. She moaned and rolled a little away from him, turning her head slightly up toward him. When she could see him through the slitted eye that was closest to the floor she winked at him with it. His eyes opened wide, then he grinned.

His face fell, "I'm so sorry you got dragged back into this. They shot one of your teammates!"

She turned her face back toward the floor and whispered, "I know, they broadcast it on the net."

Thinking about Anna's desperate struggles to avoid being shot, Ell found herself suddenly torn by conflicting emotions. She wondered what she'd been thinking to have voluntarily entered the lion's den. Yes, she was fast, but fast enough to take on *seven* armed terrorists? With handcuffs on?!

Ell gritted her teeth and took a couple of deep calming breaths. She *had* come to the lion's den, best try to pull the lion's claws, not whine about her poor decision making. She rolled her head back toward Phil, "Can you get your arms under your feet and around front?" Ell knew she could, but worried that Phil's flexibility might be limited by his muscularity.

Phil, dismayed at the tremor he heard in Ell's voice said, "I think so, but anyone who tries to do it gets a beating."

"Shut up! No talking!" One of the Arabs had come up behind them and he kicked Ell painfully in the side to punctuate his command. Phil lunged violently toward the guard. He made no contact but adequately distracted the guard from Ell. The guard started kicking Phil viciously in the back.

Phil startled Ell by grinning and winking at her before rolling face down and yelling, "Sorry, sorry!" in a piteous tone. A timbre Ell had never thought she might hear from Phil Zabrisk.

The guard tired of kicking Phil who'd started making surprisingly realistic blubbering sounds. With one more warning to "Stay quiet." The guard stalked away and Phil rolled back to give her another wink.

Ell pondered the situation. She wanted to wait a while before doing anything, just to lull the guards into lowering their attention levels. But not so long that Hamid might sacrifice another victim! Without her AI to keep time, she didn't have a good feel for how much of an hour had passed since Hamid shot Anna. Ell pulled her hands under her butt to the back of her knees and struggled up to a sitting position like most of the other athletes. Ell studied their captors, hoping for inspiration. There were seven of them, five at the front of the room near the bus and the two in the corners near the entrances. Now she could see that each of the seven had a Beretta.

Jamal made an eighth, but didn't appear to have a weapon. He sat dejectedly on the stairs in the door of the bus, shoulders sagging. Hamid must have successfully derailed Jamal's plan to leave after delivering Ell. The guard on the storm drain did indeed have a Beretta in addition to his assault rifle. It was in a holster on his right hip and she just hadn't been able to see it earlier. There were more assault rifles leaning against the bus, but only the door guard and the drain guard actually carried rifles at present. All but one of the guards carried their pistols in hip holsters rigged for right handed draw.

Ell flexed her wrists and realized that if she could get her hands in front of her she'd be able to handle a Beretta in a two hand grip with the cuffs on. But, and this seemed to be a big 'but,' how was she going to get near a guard with her hands in front of her? She pictured herself with the Beretta in her hands and then wondered if she would be able to bring herself to shoot a person, *even* someone who fully intended to kill *her*? She thought again about Anna struggling and crying piteously as Hamid lined up to shoot her. *Yes, I damn well* can *shoot these bastards!* she thought.

Then one of the athletes struggled to his feet. Ell saw that it was Michael Fentis the sprinter! A guard pulled his gun and walked over near Fentis. Stopping about six feet away, he motioned with his pistol and then followed Fentis over to the portapotty. A second guard stepped up behind Fentis and undid the cuffs while the first guard kept the gun on him from a distance. The guard opened the portapotty door so Fentis could step inside.

After a bit the portapotty door reopened. The guard re-cuffed Fentis' hands behind him and the sprinter was walked back to where he'd been sitting.

Under the cover of this activity she whispered to Phil, "I'm going to head to the portapotty in a few minutes. Can you arrange a distraction after I've been in there a minute?"

Phil stared at her round eyed. "What are you going to *do*?" he whispered back.

Ell tried to grin confidently, but felt her lip tremble a little. There'd be no way Phil would cooperate with what even *she* thought was likely a suicide mission. "I think I've got a way to get us some help. But I need a distraction for it to work. Something sexy by one of the girls would be better than one of the guys doing something threatening that got their guards up."

"What are you going to do?"

"It'd take too long to explain. Can you help?"

Phil studied her a moment then nodded and nudged the guy next to him. "Pass the word for one of the girls to do something sexy to distract the guards after Donsaii has been in the john for a minute."

That guy stared at Phil like he was out of his mind. But after a moment he turned to his left and seemed to be whispering, hopefully to pass the message on. Ell could see the wheels turning, *seemed crazy, but anything was better than sitting, waiting to die.* Ell could only hope that someone on the other side of the room would be willing to try to provide the distraction she'd asked for.

With great trepidation, Ell rolled to her stomach, put her hands behind her, then hunched up to her knees and slowly stood up, acting like it was much more of struggle than it was. She stood, swaying a little until the guard who'd kicked her earlier came over, negligently pointed his Beretta at her and motioned her toward the portapotty. She looked around as she walked, noting an open toolbox a few feet from the toilet. As with Fentis, when she arrived at the portapotty a second guard stepped up and inserted a pin into the ratchet mechanism of the plasticuffs, releasing her right wrist and leaving the cuffs dangling from her left. She stepped into the foul smelling portapotty, glad she didn't actually need to go badly enough to have to use it. She listened carefully, then leaned forward and peered out the crack in the door. The guard stood just outside the door as she had hoped, but seemed to be staring at something out of Ell's field of view. Then he yelled in a thick accent, "Sit back down until this one is done!"

Ell shifted to look to her right out the crack and saw two of the girls standing, she recognized the swimmers who had asked for her autograph that first night! They'd shrugged their jackets back off their shoulders to expose their swim suits. They were both writhing in place and Ell had to admit, they did look pretty sexy. She let the zone she'd been diligently holding off start to crash back over her.

As she felt her pulse turn to a slow throb and the world decelerate, she twisted the latch, pushing the door open. With everything moving in slow motion, the door took forever to swing back, but when it did, the guard by the potty hadn't moved. She stepped across to him and pulled the Beretta out of his holster. She found the safety and flicked it off as she stepped away from him.

First order of business was the second portapotty guard whose weapon was already drawn.

To Ell it almost seemed like someone else was directing her movements. The Beretta swung slowly up and bore vertically on the guard's right arm, so that the upward motion imparted to the muzzle by the gun's kick would only move the aim point higher on the arm, not produce a complete miss.

She squeezed the trigger, resisting the kick; the muzzle began to swing to the right while her eyes tracked the bullet to the guard's arm.

She didn't flinch as the bullet broke his humerus and grossly deformed the arm—buckling it hideously between the elbow and shoulder.

She absently noted the guard's pistol falling from nerveless fingers.

Now Ell's Beretta tracked across the left handed guard who was just beginning to react. Her finger pulled the trigger again as the muzzle passed the pistol seated in its holster on his left hip. She saw the bullet fly to strike the pistol, driving it into his hip, she saw that the unexpected impact in the middle of his turn would cause him to stumble or fall.

The gun now tracked across the guard by the door. Her finger started pulling the trigger just before it crossed the assault rifle. Yes, the gun fired as it crossed the rifle, but she saw that the bullet would miss the weapon. With great regret she squeezed the trigger again as the muzzle crossed center body mass, hoping it didn't kill.

She'd buckled her knees to lower her profile against return fire and leaned backward to present a moving target.

Her muzzle came up on Hamid, turning toward her, eyes widening, hand dropping toward his holster. His turning brought the holster on his right, opposite hip barely into view, she pulled the trigger again and saw the bullet was going to pass through his anterolateral thigh to strike the holster.

As she continued spinning, the muzzle of her Beretta passed the bus and the portapotty that'd been behind her, then passed Jamal in the door of the bus. She considered the two remaining guards who must be reacting by now.

They appeared in her field of view. Yes, they were moving, the one with the assault rifle was bringing it up and, in his excitement, fired a shot into the floor, then another. He was going to spray the athletes on automatic! The Beretta in Ell's hand fired three times as it crossed over his silhouette while his weapon also fired three more times, still hitting the floor, but each bullet tracking higher and about to point into the seated Olympians. Her muzzle tracked backwards and fired a fourth time, this bullet she saw would strike his assault weapon and drive it back, down and to the side.

She resumed turning to the right and the last guard with a weapon came into view, his hand had reached the butt of his Beretta and was pulling the weapon out of the holster. Her muzzle crossed the pistol and flared. The bullet tracked true to hit the gun and drive it into his right hip.

The guard she'd taken her gun from was stepping toward her. As her muzzle passed his thigh it flared again, she noted his thigh deforming gruesomely as the bullet struck his femur, *he'll fall,* she thought.

She continued turning. The first guard she'd shot was reaching down with his intact left arm for the weapon on the floor where his right hand had dropped it. The Beretta's muzzle flashed again, the bullet tracking correctly to strike his left arm.

The next guard was falling. As she'd predicted, he'd been caught unbalanced and unprepared for the impact of his pistol being driven into his hip. The pistol was obviously deformed from the impact. She thought, *He's out of this fight*.

Ell's eyes tracked over the door guard, still falling backward. *Yes, he's out of the fight too.*

Now she saw Hamid, gun indeed blown off his hip. Hamid was turning toward the assault rifles stacked against the bus behind him. Ell's muzzle tracked over his thighs and barked twice.

She continued tracking around the circle again. The grate guard was falling backward, his assault rifle driven back down toward the floor, no longer firing, but she worried about whether it'd shot someone already.

The seventh guard was still stumbling from the impact of his Beretta against his thigh; Ell back counted her shots, fourteen, so she had one bullet left in the Beretta if it'd had a full fifteen bullet magazine when she started. She quickly wiped it down against her pants, tossed it aside and stepped to pick up the undamaged Beretta the portapotty guard had dropped. She took it off safe.

Ell resurveyed the terrorists to make sure none of them were in condition to do harm. She looked at the athletes; they'd all hit the floor and were making themselves small.

Phil suddenly stood up. His hands in front of him, he started her way. While calling Phil's name, Ell stepped to the toolbox. She grabbed a wire cutter and tossed it toward Phil, carefully pulling the throw to make it slow enough for him to catch.

She stepped to Hamid who lay crumpled on the floor and pointed the Beretta's muzzle at his face, speaking slowly so she would be understandable, "Turn on the video link to the outside. Now!" She repeated it in case he hadn't understood.

Hamid's eyes were filled with agony and disbelief. His faced turned grim, "No! Kill me!"

Ell couldn't imagine trying to torture cooperation out of the terrorist leader. She looked over the terrorists once more to make sure none of them posed a threat, then let the zone go and felt exhaustion roll over her. Reaction trembled through her. Without a doubt she'd just seriously mangled some other human beings. Had she *killed* some of them?

Questions avalanched through her consciousness.

How would she get the police to break into the hideout to rescue them?

Could she be charged with murder for killing terrorists?

Should she go get her AI and try using the net to contact the police?

Go to the door and knock?

Was killing terrorists "justifiable homicide"?

Could she do anything to help Anna?

Should she be doing anything for the wounded terrorists?

Oh God!

She needed to get help somehow!

Suddenly it all seemed insurmountable.

Her vision blurred with tears.

The tech monitoring the audio turned, "Chief! Gunfire inside the room! Sounds like bursts of automatic weapon fire!"

Christ! They're killing them all! The chief thought to himself, "White! SWAT is go! Rip that door off and get in there before the bastards kill *all* of them!"

The assault truck started up and roared toward the door, lance extended.

Phil heard Ell call his name and saw her throw

something toward him. Reflexively he tried to catch it. HOLY HELL! It hit his bare palm like a full on baseball pitch and stung like hell! However, he did successfully catch it and looked down to recognize a wire cutter, *Ah, to cut the cable tie plasticuffs.* He couldn't turn it to cut his own cuffs, so he knelt next to the closest athlete and cut her cuffs loose, then handed her the cutters so she could cut his loose.

He thought back over what he'd just witnessed. Everyone else in the big room had been watching the two swimmers writhing and wondering *what the Hell?* Phil had been distracted momentarily, but then turned his attention back to Ell in the portapotty wondering what in the world her plan could be. The door of the portapotty had exploded out and completely off its hinges as Ell flew out. She blurred past the closest guard toward the one with the drawn pistol. Phil flinched then as an automatic weapon opened up, a muzzle flashing right in front of Ell. He expected her to be flung back, but no! It was *Ell* who'd somehow obtained a weapon and fired that burst herself. Then, she seemed to fall, spinning, back to her left. Before he could think, *She's been hit!* her spin had faced her the opposite direction and another a burst of muzzle flashes streaked to his right—just as he heard an automatic weapon start firing from over there.

As soon as Phil's wrists were free he leaped up to sprint to the front. He had no doubt that Ell's bursts had taken down two of the guards but there were seven of them! They'd be on her in a moment and his heart trip-hammered at the thought, eyes seeking one of them to tackle.

He stumbled to a halt. They were *all* down! *Holy shit!* he thought as prickles ran down his neck.

Ell! He saw her kneeling over and pointing a pistol at one of the terrorists. The man said, "Kill me!"

Distractedly Phil wondered what she'd done with her automatic weapon and where she'd gotten it, he briefly pictured it hidden in the muck at the bottom of the portapotty. But for there to be a weapon in the portapotty, someone would have had to put it in there before this even happened—so that couldn't be? Could it?

For a moment Phil wondered if she'd shoot the terrorist as he requested, but then she stood up, looking desperately around. Phil asked, "What do you need?"

"We've got to let the police know to break in here and rescue us!" She spoke so rapidly he could barely understand her; it took a moment after she stopped speaking for him to process it.

"Are they outside?" Phil asked in astonishment. "Why haven't they already broken in and rescued us?"

"This place is like a fort! It would have taken so long most of you would've been dead before they could..." Her pressured speech was interrupted by a roaring sound, then a loud crash as some long object ripped through the steel door in the corner. It deployed an enormous barb as it retracted and the door ripped outward. A moment later small objects flew through the door.

Absently, even as he saw Ell turn away, eyes scrunched shut and fingers in her ears, Phil wondered what they were. *Damn! Of course! Flash bangs!* he thought as he closed his eyes and covered his ears a moment too late to protect them from the painful sound and light. Blinded and deafened he didn't see the SWAT team members pour through the door. He wasn't really aware of them until one of the team, none too gently, shoved him down to a prone position on the floor.

Grimly, Chief Bowers followed a couple of stretchers through the small door into the terrorist hideout, expecting pandemonium and blood everywhere. To his astonishment he saw the athletes standing in a large group, talking excitedly while waiting to get their plasticuffs removed. Medics huddled over one red, white and blue uniform along one wall and by another in the middle of the room. SWAT team members stood over a number of prone or supine individuals in dark civilian clothing, mostly in the front of the room, though a couple were in the corners. Medics worked on those individuals too. He found the SWAT team leader, "Report?"

"Uh, yes sir." He pulled off his helmet and rubbed his scalp, "Two hostage casualties. The girl, shot in the abdomen during the broadcast, and one of the shot putters, shot in the ass. Looks to be a flesh wound only."

Good Christ! Bowers thought to himself. Maybe my career'll survive this fiasco after all. "The terrorists?"

"Shot to shit, sir. Most of them will make it though... Damned shame."

"What!?"

"All shot up but one sir. That Jamal guy that claimed to have turned. You know, the one we were interrogating outside?"

"What the hell!? How'd *he* get in here?!"

"Says he brought Donsaii in like we picked up on the net. *Says* it was her idea." He lifted a doubtful eyebrow.

"Shit! Is *she* in here too?" the chief asked

rhetorically. His eyes had already found her standing with the rest of the athletes. He waved off an answer, "Never mind, who shot these bastards up? We need to give 'em a medal or *something*!"

"Nobody seems to know, sir. At least whoever *does* know ain't talkin'. Maybe the bastards got in a fight with each other?"

"You're shittin' me!"

"No sir."

"Where's that boss terrorist?" The swat leader waved over toward the bus and Bowers stalked over that way. Hamid lay on the ground; one of the medics was taping an IV to his arm. His swarthy face had paled and blood soaked the thighs of his pants. "What happened, you guiding lights of the Muslim faith get in an argument with each other?"

"No! It was Donsaii! She tried to murder us! I demand an attorney."

The medic said, "You should answer the man." He moved Hamid's left leg and the terrorist gasped in pain.

"You're torturing me!" Hamid gasped.

"No sir, just trying to realign your broken legs." He nudged the right leg and Hamid gasped again. "Just not sure which way they go."

"It was Donsaii!" Hamid squeaked, "I'm telling the truth. She had a weapon and shot us all!" Hamid's jaw trembled in reaction.

The medic looked up at Bowers, "Same shit, different tune. He's sure fixated on Donsaii though. Seems to think she's Satan incarnate."

Bowers looked at Hamid musingly, "What kind of injuries these assholes got anyway?"

"This guy? Both femurs and a wound through the meat of his hip that exited through his holster and gun.

Next guy over, shot, hit his gun and knocked him on his ass. Gonna have a big damn bruise, but otherwise nothing permanent. Next guy, shot through both arms, broke both humeri. Guy by the door, left chest, right chest, probably won't make it." He pointed with his chin, "Shot in femur. Next one, also 'hit in the Beretta,' huge freakin' bruise. Must be some kinda record, four of these guys got shot in their weapons. What're the chances of that?! Guy in the corner by the storm drain is Swiss cheesed, three holes in the torso and one in his Kalashnikov, almost certainly won't make it."

A chill ran over Bowers, despite the warm air. He turned and walked over to Donsaii. "I thought I put you in protective custody."

She hung her head. "Sorry. You did. I thought I could get them to take me and let some of the other athletes go." She shook her head dejectedly, "Didn't work."

The chief grunted. "What *did* happen? How'd they all get shot up?"

She shrugged, "*I* was in the portapotty. Then there was a lot of shooting."

Bowers eyes narrowed, "The head bad guy says *you* shot them."

She looked up at the ceiling a moment, "When I came out of the portapotty I got one of their pistols." She shrugged, "When I saw they were all out of action I threatened the head guy with it. I wanted to get him to connect the camera to the net so I could call you guys to come in and rescue us. And bring medics for Anna of course."

"Anna?"

"The gymnast he shot. Anna Kernova. She's one of my teammates."

"Hmmpf." He looked away, "We'll just have to

download your AIs to find out what really went down I guess." He quickly looked back at her to see if she would be wincing as she realized he'd find out anyway.

She eyed him blandly, "Good idea chief."

Chief Bowers talked to several of the athletes who all had variations of the same story, "No, I didn't see who was shooting."

"When I heard the shooting I hit the floor."

"Donsaii? I saw her go into the portapotty right before the shooting."

"Whoever did it, tell 'em thanks!"

~~~

Back at the command truck Bowers remembered all the athletes'd had their AI's removed when they were taken captive. There wouldn't be anything to download from them. Worse, it turned out that the terrorists themselves only had very low level AIs that they pretty much used only for communication. Only two of them even had video recording, Hamid and Jamal. Jamal's was useless, when the shooting started, he dove back into the bus and it only recorded images of the floor boards. Hamid's video was facing the wrong way when the first burst went off. He began to turn toward the shooter, but apparently he was hit by a bullet and nearly knocked down. He was starting to turn back toward the shooter when the second burst of gunfire was recorded on his audio track. The Kalashnikov's distinct rip could be heard overlapping the second burst of fire, but then it cut off. Hamid's video blurred with motion artifact as it swung toward several Kalashnikovs leaning against the bus. Bowers thought he saw a figure wearing red, white and blue crouched near the
~~~

portapotty in one of the frames, then a final burst of shots apparently hit Hamid's legs and dropped him to the floor. A few moments later Donsaii could plainly be heard yelling, "Phil," and moments after that she appeared in Hamid's video log, pointing a Beretta at him and demanding that he connect her to the net. Hamid said, "No, Kill me!" and Donsaii just went away.

Bowers said, "What was that automatic weapon that shot them? I recognize the sound of a Kalashnikov on the audio at one point, but I haven't heard that other weapon before."

White from SWAT said, "The only weapons we've found so far are Beretta 9mm pistols, and the Kalashnikov assault rifles. The Arab by the storm grate had a Kalashnikov which had been fired, five rounds short of a full magazine. One of those rounds seems to have ricocheted off the floor to hit the shot putter in the butt. One of the Berettas had been fired and was fourteen rounds short of a full magazine. No other weapons had been fired. Audio records nineteen shots total, so the Beretta and the Kalashnikov account for all expended rounds."

"Wait, this Beretta'd been modified somehow to fire as an automatic weapon?"

"No sir."

"Are you saying that someone pulled a Beretta's trigger so fast it *sounded* like an automatic weapon?!"

He shrugged, "*Seems* so, sir."

"Holy crap! With bullets spraying around like that it's a miracle we don't have all sorts of collateral damage due to friendly fire! I wanted to figure out who did it so we could give them a medal. Now I'm thinking we should charge 'em with reckless endangerment!"

White wiped his forehead, "Uh, Chief. That Beretta

fired fourteen rounds. We count *exactly* fourteen rounds striking terrorists. No stray rounds. All rounds striking Arabs near the shooter hit them in the extremities or hit their *weapons*. The only rounds striking center body mass were those that hit guards thirty to forty feet away. Guards who were armed with assault rifles already in their hands. Maybe this was luck, but I think someone did this shoot purposefully and it's absolutely the finest bit of real situation shooting I've ever heard of! To be honest, Chief, I really don't think anyone *could* actually do it, so I guess it *musta'* been luck but..." He shook his head. "But if someone really *can* shoot like that, I sure want to meet 'em and make friends." He stared off to the side and muttered, "Sure as *shit* don't want to be their enemy." He looked back at Bowers, "Hey Boss, pistol shooting's an Olympic sport. Were any of the Olympians in that room on the shooting team?"

Bowers called out to one of the techs, "Gene, find out if any of the Olympians in that room were on the shooting team." Then he narrowed his eyes. "White, that gymnast Donsaii was the only non-terrorist known to be up front when this went down. She was in the portapotty. Have you seen what she did yesterday in the arena to win four gold medals?"

"Sure Chief, but there's a *huge* difference between jumping around and shooting. Has she had any weapons training?"

"She attends one of the military academies so I expect she's had some. We'll find out how much."

Gene said, "Chief? None of the athletes in that room were on any of the shooting teams. Olympic shooting events don't start for another 4 days."

Chapter Eight

The police wanted to hold the athletes for questioning and protective custody, but the athletes themselves, as well as their coaches, raised a storm of protest at this proposed disruption of the games. After all, disruption was exactly what the terrorists had wanted. By the time the police relented and let the athletes go Phil was almost late to his afternoon match. When he walked out, they had a bus waiting to take him right over to the arena and, in view of events, the wrestling officials were understanding about his late arrival. At first he worried that the morning's events would derail his concentration, but the simple expedient of imagining his opponent to be a terrorist focused his attention nicely. This resulted in a brutal takedown followed by a sudden pin of his adversary. He left the ring feeling somewhat sorry for his dazed opponent.

After a few words with his coach he was finally able to pick up his AI, put on his HUD and check what the news was saying about the terrorists. The first item he came across was an announcement, "We're relieved to report that the US Olympic athletes who were captured by terrorists have been rescued. They were for the most part uninjured except, of course, for gymnast Anna Kernova whose shooting was broadcast by the terrorists and attributed to a failure to meet their demands. Also wounded was shot putter James Olnos, struck by a stray round during the rescue. Both of the injured athletes have been taken to an undisclosed medical facility where, we are told, Ms. Kernova is currently undergoing surgery. At present no details regarding the rescue are available, though experts confess to being astonished that it was accomplished without more bloodshed amongst the athletes. The location in which they were being held has been described as 'fortress like' and we are endeavoring to learn what methods the police used to break in *so* rapidly that they were able to subdue the terrorists before they killed or maimed many, if not most, of the athletes. Apparently, almost all of the terrorists themselves were injured by gunfire and are also being removed to an undisclosed medical facility." *What the hell?* Phil thought, *how could they possibly not know that Ell rescued us?* He pulled up another webcast on gymnastics. "As you probably know by now, all the female American gymnastic athletes were among the athletes abducted by terrorists this morning and Anna Kernova, the vaulting specialist was injured. The rest of them missed their events, but officials are discussing ways for them to make up..." Someone tapped Phil on the shoulder.

When he looked up a pretty young woman, one of the guides" who escorted athletes from place to place, said, "I'm sorry Mr. Zabrisk, a couple of reporters would like to interview you. Are you able to take a few questions?"

At first Phil wondered why? Surely the low level match he'd just won didn't merit an interview? Then he realized they probably wanted to talk about the terrorists. At first reluctant, he then realized he could make sure Ell got the recognition she deserved for what she'd done. "Okay." He got up and motioned for the woman to lead the way.

When they arrived at the press area two reporters approached him. Their HUD headbands both mounted more sophisticated cameras than the standard AI equipment. "Mr. Zabrisk, you were among the athletes captured by the terrorists were you not?"

"Yes sir." Phil responded, like his military training had conditioned him.

"Were you injured in any way?"

"No sir, they kicked me some, but I get hurt a lot worse than that when I'm wrestling."

"No one seems to have any idea how the terrorists were stopped. Most of the athletes seem to agree the police arrived minutes *after* the shooting was over. Were you able to see who rescued you or what happened to set you free?"

"Yes sir. Most of the folks hit the deck when the firing started so I can see how they wouldn't have seen what happened?"

"Wait, are you saying that you *did* see what transpired?"

"Yes, sir. It was Ell Donsaii."

"*What* was Ell Donsaii?"

"She's the one that stopped the terrorists."

"What? She wasn't even there! She escaped when the bus was taken and we have video of her outside the parking deck after all you athletes had been taken down into the terrorists' fort."

"That's correct. She initially escaped, but then later came in the back way."

"Back way? We understood there were only two doors."

"Two doors and a big storm drain. She came in

through the drain. I believe she let them think they'd captured her."

"Let them think?"

"Yes sir. They dragged her in, but I think that she actually forced one of their outside accomplices bring her in."

"But why?"

"So she *could* rescue us," Phil said impatiently.

"Oh, come on now Mr. Zabrisk. Do you really believe that a sixteen year old girl intentionally allowed herself to be captured by terrorists with a plan to free the other captives?"

Phil's eyes narrowed, "Have you watched the Olympics? Do you have any idea what *that* particular sixteen year old girl can do?"

"Well yes... she is... amazing." The reporter lowered one eyebrow, "But it's a long stretch from the floor exercise to combating hardened terrorists isn't it?"

Phil colored a little. "Do you want to hear what I *saw*, or not?"

The two reporters glanced at each other with their eyes, careful not to move their heads and disturb their vid shots. "Absolutely, what *did* you see?"

"I saw," Phil ground out, "Ell Donsaii dragged into that room from the back storm drain by a couple of those Arab terrorists. I saw—her get viciously kicked for whispering to tell me that she was okay. I heard—her ask me to arrange a distraction while she was in the toilet. I saw—her get up and wait until two guards, both armed with pistols, escorted her to the portapotty in the front of the room where most of the terrorists were standing. I watched them undo her handcuffs so that she could do her business. Two of the swimmers provided the distraction she'd asked for and my friend, *my friend,* and team mate, and academy classmate." Phil realized to his dismay that he was about to get choked up and rushed to finish. "That friend, Ell Donsaii, came back out of that portapotty, moving like only Ell Donsaii can move. She took a weapon from one guard and shot them *all*. She should get a *damned* medal!"

The reporters glanced at one another again. "Can we get a copy of the vid from your AI to back this up?"

"No! They took our AIs away from us! Don't you guys even know the basic story?"

"So you're the only one that saw this?"

"I don't know. Everyone hit the floor when the shooting started. I crouched too, but I was worried about my friend Ell, so my attention was focused on her when she did what she did."

"Sooo..." The reporter's eyebrows expressed his disbelief. "*You* believe that Ms. Donsaii took a weapon from one of the terrorists and used that weapon to shoot all seven of them with no harm to herself?"

Phil lowered his voice and grated out, "I don't 'believe,' I *know*. But if you'd rather think a *fairy* appeared and shot all those Arabs with her wand, well you go ahead and believe *that*." He turned and stalked away.

***

Yousef stared out the window of the office they'd rented for him and wondered what'd gone wrong? Everything had seemed to be going perfectly. The police were stymied outside and Hamid had been in complete control of the situation. Yousef had watched with enormous satisfaction as Hamid had made his demands. Yousef'd been daunted by the rapidity with which the police had arrived, cordoned off the area, brought in vehicles and prepared themselves. The assault vehicle that'd rolled down the ramp into the building had looked very intimidating, but, as Hamid had predicted, the heavy concrete walls must have been too much to breach without severe risks to the hostages.

Yousef had greatly enjoyed watching the American girl's struggles before Hamid shot her. Though he'd been disappointed when Hamid didn't finish her off, he'd understood the increased pressure her wounds put on the Americans and admired Hamid for recognizing that factor. At first Yousef hadn't been able to believe it when Hamid told him over the intercom that Jamal'd brought in Donsaii, but it'd seemed to be further proof that Allah was on their side.

Then, over the intercom he'd heard several bursts of automatic weapons fire. Like Chief Bowers, he'd thought that the Americans had rebelled and Hamid's team was putting the dogs down with their assault rifles. Yousef felt a frisson of delight at the thought of their broken bodies, shattered by the weapons. But then to his dismay he heard Hamid say "No! Kill me!" Then several loud bangs and much shouting ensued. Later he distinctly heard Hamid say, "It was Donsaii! She tried to murder us all!"

Evidently, all their plans'd come apart. He watched the ambulances enter and leave the parking deck. Then, with mounting disappointment he saw the American athletes come out of the deck in small groups and get into vans and buses. They came out in fits and starts so it was a little hard to keep track, but he thought he'd counted all but two or three of the hostages. They all walked out on their own!

When the police began breaking down their equipment and leaving, Yousef realized that his team's grand gesture was not just finished, but sadly dismembered.

However, the Americans didn't have Yousef! He could still make them pay!

Yousef knew he wasn't a great planner, but even if he merely killed some people at the Olympic facility, the fear it would generate would be a thorn in the side of the great Satan. He un-taped his Beretta and its two spare mags from the bottom of the office desk. He put the Berretta in the waistband of his pants, dropped the mags in his oversized left front pocket and pulled the baggy t-shirt down over it.

He walked down the hall to the bathroom and inspected his appearance. The weapons weren't evident and for a moment he was thankful for the loose clothing that was in style here in America. He went down the stairs and started walking to the Olympic facilities. He knew he wouldn't be able to get in with his weapons, but he would just wait outside for Donsaii to leave, then kill her and as many other Americans as possible.

***

Coach Benson was beside herself. Ell had arrived in the gymnastics area dressed like a spectator with a ball cap covering her signature hair. At first the coach was ecstatic that her star gymnast *had* arrived to compete, but then Ell had told the coach she just didn't want to participate any more. "But Ell, I got them to give special permission for you to do your all around events this afternoon! You could get another couple of gold medals! You're gonna knock 'em dead!"

Ell winced at Benson's choice of terms, but continued staring at the floor. "Sorry Coach, just don't feel up for it. Be good for someone else to get a gold medal anyway, four's enough for me." Her thoughts returned to an incessant cycling through the shooting. Her mind's eye riding once again behind the barrel of the Beretta as it traveled the big concrete room. Over and over she tracked the fusillade of bullets fired from *her* weapon.

~~~

"But Ell!" Benson paused, "Did you get hurt?"

"No Coach," her voice sounded flat and lifeless, "Just not happy about what happened."

"Are you worried about Anna? I'm told she's out of surgery and expected to do well."

"I'm glad coach." Ell stood and turned away. She couldn't tell the coach about it, but she had to talk to someone. "I'm gonna go find my Gram and my Mom."

Coach Benson followed behind her a few steps, then turned her palms up, shrugged and turned away. For a moment she wondered where Ell had obtained the vaguely uniform-like blue pants and shirt she had on over her leotard. Surprising really, that Ell would be the one who couldn't take the events of the morning. The other girls seemed much flightier. Benson could understand being terrified after being held hostage, but giving up years of effort toward Olympic gold? Without even being injured? Without at least giving it a try? She shook her head, then resolutely turned her attention
~~~

back to the rest of her team. They still needed her.

Ell queried her AI. Allan located Ell's Gram and her Mom back at the room that'd been rented for them. They'd been to the parking deck during the crisis, then when Ell had been bussed directly to the Olympic center they'd begun to follow her there. But, apparently Gram had been overcome by the excitement started feeling dizzy and nauseous. Kristen had taken her back to the room.

Ell had Allan message them that she was coming to the hotel and started for the main entrance to the complex. Then she heard Phil's voice in the distance behind her, "Ell, wait up." She turned and saw the big blond man trotting her way. She wasn't sure she wanted to talk to him, but she stopped and waited. When Phil caught up, he stopped, stared at her for a second then threw his arms around her. "Ell! I'm so sorry I didn't get to say 'thanks' earlier. When they put me on the bus to come over here for my match they had you sequestered somewhere."

He squeezed her so hard she wondered if he knew what he was doing to her ribs.

But the hug felt wonderful.

She put her arms around his broad back and squeezed him back. She leaned back a little, "Thanks for what?" she asked with a trembling lip. On one hand she hoped that he, like the others, didn't know the terrible things she'd done in that room. On the other hand, she desperately wanted a friend to talk it out with.

"For taking those bastards out! I and every other person in that room owe you our lives!" To his dismay Phil saw her eyes fill with tears.

Ell buried her face into his broad chest. "Oh Phil! I think I might have *killed* two of them!"

Phil leaned his head back to look down at her, not at all sure what to say in response to that. "They *deserved* a lot more than a kick in the nuts, you know?"

She leaned back and grinned crookedly up at him through her tears. "You're *never* gonna let me live that down are you?"

"Actually, my greatest fear is that you'll tell my friends about the day you kicked my ass. Ruin my reputation."

Ell put her face back into his chest and snuffled, "You *have* friends?"

He squeezed again, "The one that matters most is you." One hand rose to muss her hair. "Can I take you somewhere? People are starting to stare."

Ell peered past his pectoral and saw a crowd had gathered to watch an Olympic athlete hugging someone, but now some of them were pointing at her and she saw one mouthing "Donsaii," so evidently they were seeing through her police officer disguise. She wiped her eyes on the front of his jacket and said, "Yes, take me to my Mom's hotel." He dropped the hug, turned them both back toward the main entrance and, to her surprise, took her left hand in his right.

~~~

The two reporters who had interviewed Phil earlier had been walking along behind him, not following him, just discussing other possible interviews. He'd jogged ahead of them and they'd lost sight of him, but then they came up on him again, stopped, hugging a young woman. They'd stopped to watch, wondering if there was a story here? At first, like most of the crowd, they were only looking at the big, good looking Olympic athlete. But then they noticed that the girl had
~~~

strawberry blond hair peeking out from under her hat. She seemed to be sobbing, then she leaned back. It was *Donsaii!* Zabrisk and the girl started walking toward the entrance. Most of the crowd respected their emotional state by drawing back to let them go, but the reporters followed.

That was their job and this seemed like it could be a great interview!

As Phil and Ell opened a door to go outside into the heat, the reporters jogged a few more steps to catch up and one of them called out, “Mr. Zabrisk, Ms. Donsaii, can we have a couple minutes of your time?”

Ell shrank inside herself, but Phil picked up their pace, turned over his shoulder and gruffly said, “Leave her alone!”

The reporters trailed behind, undeterred. “Ms. Donsaii, Mr. Zabrisk says you’re the one responsible for rescuing the athletes. Is that true?”

Phil flinched as Ell darted a wide eyed look up at him. He grimaced and whispered, “I thought you’d *want* the world to know. *I* would. I’m so, so, sorry.”

Ell pulled her hand out of his and turned her eyes to the front, but continued to walk alongside him. One of the reporters again said, “Ms. Donsaii?” A movement up ahead caught her attention. A man who’d been leaning against a car in the large parking lot outside the arena stood up and stared at her. Initially she thought he was Hispanic, but then, looking at his nose, she thought he might be Arabic. His right hand reached down and lifted the hem of his oversized t-shirt, then grasped his waistband, though it didn’t bring anything out. Ell had slowed, causing Phil to look back over his shoulder at her. The reporter caught up and touched her right elbow, thinking that she was slowing for him.

Impatiently, Ell shrugged his touch away as if were an insect. The Arabic man's eyes narrowed, then his arm jerked convulsively as he pulled a Beretta out of his waistband. Ell felt the zone crash over her once again!

As her world slowed, Ell took note of the crowd of bodies around her. She looked down for something to throw at the man whose Beretta had cleared his shirt, but she saw nothing but concrete and pavement.

In her slowed world she considered running at the man, but discarded that as hopeless. Fast as she was, he'd get off several shots.

The reporter who'd touched her elbow had gone past her a step on her right when Ell paused. She saw the heavy battery for his AV equipment hanging on his belt clip.

The Arab's pistol came up.

Ell's right hand pulled the battery off the reporter's belt, left hand snaking out to rip the jacked wire off its top.

Ell glimpsed the bore of the Beretta as it swung up, but then for a moment it swung too high.

Ell's arm cocked back, battery in hand as her left foot slid ahead, lowering her stance.

The Beretta barked, Ell saw the bullet would miss her slightly high and to her right. The kick had driven his muzzle up.

She focused on the shooter's right shoulder and swung the battery forward.

The Beretta lowered and barked a second time as Ell released the battery. Ell saw the shot was wild, but realized that, even though the shots would miss her, they would almost certainly hit someone behind her.

She lunged to pull another battery off the reporter's belt, but then saw the first battery clip the terrorist's thumb, knocking the pistol wide before tumbling up the length of his arm to glance off his forward thrust shoulder. It struck his collarbone and thudded solidly into his neck.

The man flew backwards and sprawled onto the pavement, gun tumbling from his splayed fingers.

Ell sprinted forward, swiveling her head in search of more men with guns or Arabic phenotypes. She snatched up the Beretta and, still moving, spun around with it extended and tracking 360.

Seeing no one, she safed the pistol, asked Allan to call in the incident to the police and turned to be sure that the terrorist posed no further threat. He lay on the ground, right arm sprawled out bonelessly and left hand grasping his neck. The man was hoarsely gasping out Arabic phrases.

Allan told her the man was cursing but didn't translate exactly what he was saying.

Ell did another 360 and then let the zone go. She turned to peer at the crowd to see who'd been hurt. Some of the crowd stood stunned, many crouched or were down flat like you would expect in the face of gunfire. It was hard to see if anyone was hurt. "Phil! How many injured?"

Phil closed his mouth and looked around him. A man and a woman in the area behind where Ell had been were on their backs. The rest of the people were down on their stomachs. He stepped back to them and saw blood. "Two," he shouted, kneeling to look at the victims. The man was holding his stomach and the woman her shoulder. Both looked pale and frightened. Phil pulled off his jacket and wadded it up, placing it on the man's stomach, "Hold this." Phil stood and stripped off his sweatpants and knelt to press them to the woman's wound.

A woman stepped up and said, "I'm a surgeon, may I help?"

Puzzled to be asked permission, Phil looked up in gratitude and said, "Please!" he heard sirens in the distance. The surgeon knelt, told Phil and another bystander to lift the victims' legs and began asking questions.

Having learned from her first experience that she shouldn't be holding a weapon when the police arrived, Ell knelt and put the safed Beretta on the ground when the first police car came into view. She placed it far from the terrorist and started back to the crowd on the walkway. She knelt by the two wounded and turned to each, saying, "I'm so sorry. So, so sorry." Her eyes filled with tears again.

The man grimaced up at her, "Did *you* shoot me?"

"Oh! No! But the man that hit you was shooting at me and missed."

"You're Ell Donsaii aren't you?"

Ell, surprised at this non-sequitur, snuffled. Her voice cracked, "Yes sir."

The man grimace-grinned and said, "Sign an autograph for my son and I'll let you off the hook for ducking."

Ell grinned crookedly through her tears, sniffed again and said, "Yes sir," and looked around for something to sign with. Someone in the crowd held out a pen and a card. Ell took it and placed it on her knee, "What's your son's name?"

As Ell finished signing the autograph she heard a policeman step up behind her. "Who saw what happened here?"

The reporter said, "The guy in the parking lot started

shooting at Ms. Donsaii."

Ell looked up to see the policeman glance at her then look over at the terrorist, still sprawled on the pavement with a few spectators around him and another policeman kneeling beside him. "Who shot the guy?" He turned slowly to let his cameras pan the scene.

"Um, you might not believe this, but Ms. Donsaii threw one of my batteries at him. I should have video to document."

"Come on! He's wounded! He's coughing up blood and having trouble breathing!"

"Nothing else touched the guy. There weren't any shots fired other than the two he fired himself."

Medics arrived with stretchers for the two victims, started IVs and loaded them up, the surgeon following them to the ambulance.

The cop looked around then focused on the reporter. He barked a laugh and said, "Sure, send me video, but sure as shit, *someone* shot that dude."

More police arrived, cordoned off the area and didn't let people leave until they'd been asked a few questions, transferred the video from their AIs and had given their contact info.

Chief Bowers watched the reporter's video as he rode to the site of the new incident. The first thing he noticed was that the reporter was a pain in the ass, bugging Donsaii even though she obviously didn't want to be approached. The chief didn't see the terrorist or notice him lean away from the car and focus on Donsaii the first time through the video. The second time in slow-mo, it was obvious that Donsaii saw the guy immediately. She reacted instantaneously, slowing and then at the same time that the terrorist pulled out a

Beretta, she lunged for the battery. She threw the battery at the terrorist like it was a fast pitch softball. On the first run through the video Bowers thought some kind of glitch caused the vid to speed up when Donsaii blurred into motion. On the second viewing in slow motion he noticed that everything else moved normally, only Ell was moving so fast it was hard to follow. He thought, *My God! That girl's faster than anyone ever dreamed possible!* He watched the battery rocket across the lot and strike the terrorist along the shoulder, tumbling down his collarbone and across his neck, hurling him off his feet. In slow motion the battery created a huge trough in the terrorist's flesh, followed by waves racing over his flesh.

Waves like a rock created in the water when it dropped in a pond.

After seeing the video, he wasn't surprised to receive a call telling him the terrorist had arrived at the hospital DOA. Later he'd learn that the terrorist had a broken thumb and two broken ribs, but the fatal injuries included "laceration of the subclavian artery by the clavicle" and "severe trauma to the larynx."

The chief watched the reporter's video of Zabrisk claiming that Donsaii had been the one to take out all the terrorists down in their redoubt. He shook his head and re-watched his own interview with her.

He heard himself say, "What *did* happen? How'd they all get shot up?"

She shrugged, "I was in the portapotty. Then there was a lot of shooting."

"The head bad guy says you shot them."

She glanced up at the ceiling a moment, "When I came out of the portapotty I got one of their pistols." She shrugged, "When I saw they were all out of action I threatened the head guy with it. I wanted to get him to connect the camera to the net so I could call you guys to come in and rescue us. And bring medics for Anna of course."

Damn! He thought. She didn't lie to me. She just didn't say that she was the one that took them "out of action!" He snorted a laugh at himself, And, since I didn't consider it to be a possibility, I didn't ask any followup questions!

~~~

Kristen and her mother were still in their room. When an hour passed and Ell hadn't come to their room—as she'd messaged that she would—they started to worry. Before they got frantic another message told them that she'd be "held up a while." They wondered if she'd changed her mind and decided to compete in the gymnastic events after all. However, when they went on the net to see if there was anything about her competing, they were astonished that the first item her name pulled up was a terrorist shooting outside the arena! With increasing dismay they watched a video in which a man shot at Ell and then, without surprise in view of Ell's history with attackers, they saw her *take him out of play.* They were horrified to hear of the injuries to the people behind Ell. However, they were almost overwhelmed when they learned that Ell had been the one who'd stopped the terrorists and set the athletes free earlier in the day.

Ell's grandmother said, "She's going to be really upset. Remember how freaked out she was when she blinded the guy that attacked you?"

"Yeah, and even though she hates Jake, she was really distressed when she broke his arm. This is gonna
~~~

tear her up. *She* won't see herself as a hero."

They listened to the news services laud their little girl, "We've learned that four time gymnastic gold medalist Ell Donsaii was responsible for the rescue of the US Olympic athletes captured by terrorists earlier today. Despite watching her impossible gymnastic feats yesterday, it remains difficult to countenance the reports of her taking a pistol from one of the terrorists and using it to subdue seven hardened extremists. However, the video that follows is from another terrorist attempt this afternoon and shows just how decisively and rapidly this girl can respond in the face of horrific circumstances. In this video you see her use the amazing physical quickness that won Olympic gold to subdue a man who was shooting at her—by throwing a videographer's battery at him! So, though we don't have video documentation of her rescue of the other athletes from the terrorists, this makes it seem plausible."

They were still watching report after report at seven in the evening when a knock came on their door. When they opened it Ell stood there with a large, good looking young man. "Oh Ell," Kristen threw her arms around her. "I'm so glad you're okay!"

Ell's grandmother stepped up and put her arms around both of them and they all degenerated into tears as they shuffled into the room. After they quieted down to snuffles Kristen asked, "Who's this young man?" she indicated Phil with her chin, "Have they assigned you a guard or something?"

"No Ma'am, I'm one of her teammates. Your daughter's been protecting *me* today, not the reverse, and I *surely* do appreciate it."

"You're a gymnast? You're awfully big."

Phil chuckled. "No, Ma'am, I'm a wrestler."

Haltingly, Ell told them an edited version of how she and Phil met and how they were at the Academy together and were now at the Olympics together. When she saw speculation rising in her Gram's eyes she quickly said, "We're friends, Gram. Very, very good friends, but he's *not* my boyfriend."

~~~

Though Phil would have described their relationship the same way, he found he was sore disappointed to be "*not* my boyfriend." He turned to them and said with a husky voice, "She saved my life. I owe her *everything*. If she ever decides she *does* need a boyfriend, I'll be on deck, waiting." He was saved from getting completely choked up by a knock on the door. He got up and headed that way.

He heard them asking, "Who could that be?" though they let him answer it.

Shortly he returned with a couple large boxes. At their wide eyes he shrugged, "I was hungry so I ordered pizza. There's enough for all of us."

As they laughed and fell to eating, the conversation became more cheerful. After the pizza was gone there was another knock at the door. Phil answered the door again, this time returning with Chief Bowers. They all stood, but he made little downward pushing motions with his hands, "No, no, sit. Please, sit."

They sat and invited the Chief to sit as well. After settling himself, he twisted his hat in his hands a moment, harrumphed and said, "I find myself in the mind of a man going out to close the barn door after the horses have already fled... And also of the mind of a man setting out a dog to protect his lion..." He paused
~~~

long enough that they were about to ask him what he meant, then, "I feel I've let you down Ms. Donsaii. Twice, in fact. My job is to protect the citizens of this fair city and especially lately, you athletes. First I failed by letting those terrorists get set up here in Dallas. After you saved me from disgrace on that issue, I then failed to consider that some of them might remain on the loose." He gave her a nod, "Thank you for saving my bacon on that one too." He dropped his eyes to the floor.

Ell said, "Chief, I don't know how you could have known…"

"It's my job to know. Admittedly it's a hard job, but it's what I signed up for and I'm disappointed that I failed. I wanted to tell you I'm sorry. I also want to tell you just how much I admire you for showing up in my command center and offering to be traded to the terrorists for your team mates." Everyone in the room turned to stare at Ell on that note. "I thought you were just such a good person that you were willing to trade your life for theirs. I still think it's amazing that you were willing to *risk* your life for theirs, though now I realize that you truly did believe that you could help free them. And in fact, when I refused to trade you, Jamal Assad tells me you talked him into conducting you to their back entrance?"

"Um, yes sir," Ell said, blushing.

"So you *did* then intentionally put your life at risk for the others. You have my greatest admiration, and I fully intend to put you up for the highest medal that fits, though I don't really think there's one high enough to match what you did today."

"Chief, I've got plenty of medals." Ell said quietly, eyes on the floor. "And I'm *not* proud of shooting those people."

He grimaced, "Well, that's true. But if I have my way you're gonna get another one, and I hope to be the one to pin it on you."

In a small voice Ell said, "But, I really don't want any more attention."

"I think your nation *needs* to recognize a real hero, and you're just the one to be recognized."

Her mom hugged her as the chief continued. "As to the dog I'm setting out to protect the lion, I'm posting two guards in your hall. Though I fear that if someone does attack, you might wind up saving them." The chief's eyes lost focus a moment as he listened to his AI. "Yes, of course I'll speak to him. Yes sir. Yes sir, this is Chief Bowers. Yes sir, I'm with her now. Just a minute sir, I'll ask." He focused on Ell, "You have your AI blocking all calls?"

"All but family," she said with a grimace, wondering who was trying to get through now. She'd gotten so many contacts from reporters and news agencies since the second attack that she'd blocked all but close family. All of her first degree relatives were with her in the room.

"Would you make an exception for the President?"

"President of what?"

The chief grinned. "These United States, I believe he's your Commander in Chief?"

"Um, yes sir." She sat up straighter and focused straight ahead as she heard the well known voice of President Teller in her headset. "Yes sir... Yes sir... Thank you sir... I appreciate that sir... Yes sir, I do have one request... That Jamal Assad be given asylum and put into the witness protection program for his help today... Yes sir, thank you sir."

Chief Bowers said, "Sir, I would like to nominate her for the highest civilian medal there is... Uh yes sir, I do know that she is a member of the military, it'd just slipped my mind... Yes sir, I do agree that the Medal of Honor would be appropriate, the terrorists were indeed 'enemies of these United States.'"

~~~

When the call was concluded Phil burst out, "I'm gonna have to salute you?! That's going a little far!"

Ell, currently being hugged tightly by her mother and grandmother said, "What?

"Everyone, no matter their rank, is supposed to salute Medal of Honor winners!" He paused, then rose to his feet, said, "What the hell!" came to attention and rendered a sharp regulation salute. "At least I'll be able to say I was first," he grinned at her.

Ell squeaked as her mom hugged harder, "But I haven't got it yet!" she whispered.

Chief Bowers rose to his feet and said, "You *will*, and I'll be able to say I saluted you second." He rendered a sharp military salute. "Semper Fi! Hope you don't mind getting a salute from an old Marine?" he said with a twinkle in his eye.

After a lot more hugs, tears, smiles and back patting, Phil took his leave, as did the Chief. The Chief paused to introduce them to the guards he'd set in the hall as he went out. Ell and her mom and Gram talked for many hours alone, Ell appreciating the chance to vent her agony over having killed the guard by the drain, the man in the parking lot, and doing serious harm to so many others. Even though she could abstractly agree that they deserved what they'd received, she *hated* having been the one to mete out that punishment.
~~~

Eventually Ell went to bed in her mom's room. Unable to sleep, she laid awake staring at the ceiling, endlessly rehashing the events of the day. Ultimately she resorted to her practice of considering possible mathematical descriptions of her postulated small dimension through which entangled particles and double slit photons were connected. As she drifted off, her scalp abruptly prickled when she realized that the odd mathematical convention she'd just tried actually *did* fit the known data she'd been trying to tie together! She sat bolt upright, then spent hours recording and reordering formulas and having Allan run them against known experimental data pulled in off the net. It was nearly dawn before she got to sleep, grateful that the math breakthrough had taken her mind off the trauma of the day.

Epilogue

Most of a year had passed since that fateful second day at the Dallas Olympics. President Teller had agreed to give the commencement speech at the Air Force Academy. After Teller had spoken and the cadets had received their diplomas in the traditional fashion, the Commandant of the Academy said, "Now I have the privilege of turning the podium back over to the President of the United States. Mr. President?"

The President stepped back to the podium. "I am sure that most of you will not be surprised to find that my next words have something to do with a most unusual cadet that you have amongst your ranks." He looked out over the assembled cadets, "Ms. Donsaii, I believe 'front and center' is the usual command at such times?"

Everyone waited patiently as Ell got up from her seat out in the audience and marched her way to the front. She approached the podium and to her surprise she suddenly recognized Chief Bowers and Jamal Assad seated among the dignitaries on the stage! Despite a mental hiccough she turned smoothly and saluted the President.

He returned the salute, then turned back to the audience and cameras. "I'm sure you're all aware that, before her participation was interrupted by a terrorist attack, Ms. Donsaii won *four* back to back individual

gold medals in Gymnastics at the Olympic Games last summer." He paused for thunderous applause to surge up and gradually die out.

"Unless you were living under a rock, I'm sure you are also aware of the role she played in frustrating the plans of those terrorists. After escaping to warn us, she purposefully allowed herself to be recaptured by the terrorists and then single handedly killed or disabled eight extremists, thus saving the lives of twenty-eight Team USA athletes including one of your fellow cadets and Olympic Silver Medalist, Mr. Phillip Zabrisk." The President paused again for tumultuous cheering to rise up and then gradually subside.

"Today I am proud to announce that, in the name of the Congress of the United States, I am awarding Ms. Donsaii the Medal of Honor 'for conspicuous gallantry and intrepidity at the risk of her life, above and beyond the call of duty, while engaged in action against an enemy of the United States.'" He picked up a case from the podium, opened it and pulled out a ribbon with the medal on it. He held it up to the crowd for a moment, then turned to put it around Ell's neck. Turning back to the microphone he said. "I believe the tradition is that everyone, regardless of rank or status, is encouraged to salute Medal of Honor winners. I wish to be first to do so." He made a creditable left face and rendered Ell a sharp military salute.

Out in the audience Phil elbowed Jason, "Actually, I was the first," he whispered.

The President turned back to the microphone, "Company... ten hut!" With a crash the military personnel on the stage and in the audience stood and came to attention. He turned again to Ell and said, "Present arms," and he, as well as all the military

personnel present rendered their sharpest salutes. "At ease, and please be seated.

"Now I suppose you might think that we have rendered Ms. Donsaii sufficient honors for one day. However, there are a few things that you probably *aren't* aware of. Ms. Donsaii is not only a physical phenom, able to perform athletically at a level no one had really dreamed possible, but she is undeniably a genius as well. By now most of you are aware that the Academy's rules were bent to allow her to enter at the unheard of age of fifteen. *Some* of you may be aware that when she entered, she essentially tested out of most of the first two years of the academic curriculum here at the Academy. A very few of you are aware, though many of you will be unsurprised to learn, that she has completed the remainder of the academic coursework requirements for graduation in the two years that she has been here. The girl is still under the age of eighteen!

"Furthermore, I am able to announce that today the prestigious scientific journal Nature is publishing a paper that she submitted. A paper entitled 'A Possible Mechanism for Quantum Entanglement through an Unperceived Dimension.' I am assured by those who understand this science, that this paper will stir up the world of physics like very few papers since the publications of Albert Einstein more than a century ago."

The complete stunned silence of the audience was palpable. The President grinned and reached into the podium again. "Thus it is my distinct, if unusual, privilege to award one more graduation diploma today, two years earlier than expected, to Ms. Ell Donsaii. And to inform her that she has offers from MIT, Cal Tech and

numerous other schools to enter their graduate programs in physics. I also inform her that her country believes it's in the best interest of these United States that she attend such a graduate school prior to serving her time on active duty." He turned to Ell and handed her the diploma, then saluted her once again, holding it while she returned the salute. They both held their salutes until he whispered, "I'm holding this salute until you drop yours first." He winked. She dropped her salute and the stadium erupted.

The End

Hope you liked the book!

Try the next in the series, "Smarter (an Ell Donsaii Story #2)"

To find other books by the author try Laury.Dahners.com/stories.html

Author's Afterword

This is a comment on the "science" in this science fiction novel. I've always been partial to science fiction that posed a "what if" question. Not everything in the story has to be scientifically possible, but you suspend your disbelief regarding one or two things that aren't thought to be possible. Essentially you ask, what if

something (such as faster than light travel) were possible, how might that change our world? Each of the Ell Donsaii stories asks at least one such question.

"Quicker" asks, what if an individual had a mutation allowing faster nerve transmission than the rest of us? Our nerves send their messages along axons, which are incredibly long processes that stick out of the main body of the nerve cell. Some of these axons are several feet long (from your spinal cord to your toes). Conduction of messages along these axons aren't very fast unless the axons are coated with myelin, a coating that allows the message to "skip' from one node to the next along the surface of the axon. An example of the difference in conduction speeds between myelinated and unmyelinated fibers (that you might have experienced yourself) occurs when you smash a finger. When the hammer first hits your finger, you feel the "thump" which is conducted along myelin coated sensory axons. The pain comes a few seconds later when the unmyelinated pain fibers conduct that sensation up to your brain at their slower rate. So a mutation that made you faster would need to affect the myelin, rather than the neurons themselves, perhaps by making the nodes that the messages jump along farther apart.

However, for Ell to be able to move faster than the rest of us, she must also have powerful muscles capable of moving her limbs more quickly than our muscles do. It is recognized that we all have both "fast twitch" muscle fibers that move quickly, but have little endurance and "slow twitch" muscles that move more slowly and have better endurance. For the purposes of these stories, Ell inherited a tendency for a much higher proportion of very powerful fast twitch fibers from her

athletic parents. As well, her father passed a gene variant to her that had given him much stronger and faster fast twitch fibers than the rest of us.

Thus Ell's nerves conduct messages much more quickly to her limbs which can move very rapidly because they have a very high proportion of extraordinarily powerful fast twitch fibers. For this capability she's sacrificed stamina because she has a low proportion of the slow twitch fibers needed for endurance sports like distance running.

It's been argued that humans cannot become more intelligent because, if we put more neurons in our skull, they'll be farther apart. This would slow down our thought processes because communication among neurons over those distances would be slow (i.e. giant headed aliens from SF movies might be smart, but would think very slowly). But Ell's new myelin mutation makes the coating on the axons thinner. Therefore, with less myelin in her brain, there is more room in her skull for extra neurons that can be close together. This, in combination with the faster transmission rates, provides her with more and faster processing that results in her genius level intelligence.

So, we have a novel exploring the question, "What if a young woman was extraordinarily quick, well-coordinated and intelligent?"

Acknowledgements

I would like to acknowledge the editing and advice of Gail Gilman, Elene Trull and Nora Dahners, each of

whom significantly improved this story.